St. Elizabeth's Children's Hospital, London

Dealing with sick kids can be heartbreaking,
funny and uplifting, often all at once!

This series takes a look at a hospital set up
especially to deal with such children,
peeping behind the scenes into almost all the
departments and clinics, exploring the problems,
treatments and cures of various diseases,
while watching the staff fall helplessly in love—
with the kids and with each other.

Enjoy!

Gill Sanderson is a psychologist who finds time to write only by staying up late at night. Weekends are filled by her hobbies of gardening, running and mountain walking. Her ideas come from her work, from one son who is an oncologist, one son who is a nurse and her daughter, who is training to be a midwife. She first wrote articles for learned journals and chapters for a textbook. Then she was encouraged by her husband, an established writer of war stories, to change to fiction.

SECOND LOVER
Gill Sanderson

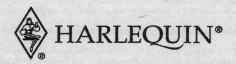

HARLEQUIN®

TORONTO • NEW YORK • LONDON
AMSTERDAM • PARIS • SYDNEY • HAMBURG
STOCKHOLM • ATHENS • TOKYO • MILAN • MADRID
PRAGUE • WARSAW • BUDAPEST • AUCKLAND

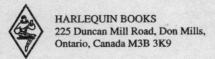

HARLEQUIN BOOKS
225 Duncan Mill Road, Don Mills,
Ontario, Canada M3B 3K9

ISBN 0-373-63162-6

SECOND LOVER

First North American Publication 2001

Copyright © 2000 by Gill Sanderson

CHAPTER ONE

IT WAS the walk Lyn first noticed.

It was the start of the day at Lizzie's—St Elizabeth's Children's Hospital—and the glassed-in entryway was thronged with visitors, hurrying staff, ancillary workers, parents with or without children. All were walking purposefully, minding their own business. But this woman's walk was wrong.

She walked quickly, her steps gradually increasing in speed. Then she would glance behind her and her pace would slow, as if she was forcing herself to be calm. Lyn shrugged. This was a hospital; there were a hundred reasons for people to act slightly oddly. But still she watched as the woman came towards her.

The woman was carrying a baby—a neonate, Lyn guessed. Most mothers carried their new babies cautiously, but this one nearly tripped as she moved over the pavement, and her pace didn't slow. It was a warm September day but the woman was wearing a long mac, buttoned up to the neck. There was nothing really wrong, but...

By now the woman was almost facing her. Deliberately Lyn stood in her way and peered at the tiny pink face in the bundle the woman was grasping so tightly. 'What a lovely baby,' she said. 'Is he—or she—?'

'I haven't time to talk,' the woman snapped. 'Excuse me.' Then she was round Lyn and moving more quickly than ever.

Lyn looked up at the grey-brick façade of Lizzie's. This

5

was to be her first day here, as senior house officer in the neurology department. She had felt so pleased to get the position, for she knew there had been considerable competition for it. She was anxious to do well. And how many times had she been told in her training—don't make assumptions, don't rush in, investigate before taking any action? Ask, wait, check and double-check. But...

Lyn turned to watch the woman, and frowned. Under the long coat the woman was wearing some kind of light, shapeless trousers—they could be hospital scrubs, in fact. She made for an illegally parked red car, opened the door and, after a wild glance behind her, thrust the baby into some kind of cot on the floor behind the front seat. There was no attempt at settling the child, no signs of tucking in, making sure it was comfortable. The woman darted round to the driver's door and seconds later the car pulled jerkily into the traffic. She hadn't fastened her safety belt.

Lyn thought she was probably panicking, making a fool of herself for no reason. But there was a one-per-cent chance that she wasn't. She had to take a chance.

She glanced at the traffic-filled main road, where a taxi had just drawn up, and a man and a baby climbed out. Another man with a small family was waving at the taxi, smiling as he walked towards it. Lyn ran up the pavement, got to the open door just before the man, and leaped inside. 'Sorry,' she said. 'Medical emergency, I'm a doctor, I'm sure you don't mind.' From his angry face she guessed he probably did mind, but she had already slammed the door.

The cab eased out into the traffic. 'Can you follow that red car that's just ahead?' Lyn asked the cabbie.

The man turned to squint at her. 'You've been watching too many films, love. What d'you think I am?'

'This is a medical emergency,' Lyn said, repeating the

phrase as if it were a spell. 'I'm a doctor. Look, here's my badge.' Fortunately she had been issued with the hospital identity badge some days ago.

The cabbie turned and stared at the badge. 'All right. But I'm going to have to report this.'

'Please do. Look, she's getting away!'

The cab driver eyed the morning London traffic, bumper to bumper, wheel arch to wheel arch. 'No chance of a fast car chase in this, love. We'll just cruise along nicely behind her; she can't get far. What's all this about?'

'I'll tell you later.' Lyn shut the partition and sat back, trying to relax. What should she do next? Her first day at the hospital, and she was probably making an almighty fool of herself. There was only one person she could say she really knew there, and that was Henry Birkinshaw, the consultant whose firm she had joined, who was even now waiting to welcome her to her new job. So be it. Henry would have to know. She took out her mobile phone, got through to the hospital and asked for his extension.

'Extension 793.' It wasn't Henry who answered the phone. Henry's voice was like Henry the man; clear, precise, pedantic. This voice was slower, almost drawling. There was perhaps a hint of a West country accent; it was a comfortable voice. What a time to be dreaming about voices! She had to be exact, for the last thing she needed was to cause a panic.

'I am Lyn Webster, Henry Birkinshaw's new senior house officer. Who am I talking to, please?'

The voice was amused. 'I am Ross McKinnon, one of Henry Birkinshaw's two specialist registrars. Henry's sorting out a problem on the ward. I just popped in to meet you, Lyn, and help welcome you to the firm. Any problem? Going to be late?'

His voice invited confidence; he would be good with children. Stop it! She had to be exact. 'Dr McKinnon, I think I'm making a fool of myself. I'm in a taxi, following a woman in a car. I saw her walking out of the hospital and I wondered if she...if she had stolen the baby.' Now she had actually said it, the very idea sounded ridiculous. Then something came back to her—perhaps a reason for her subconscious to be on the alert. 'Remember that case in north London last week?'

He did. 'A woman was disturbed on a ward, and nearly got away with a neonate. Yes, we heard. Our security man suggested a few more precautions. It would be very hard to steal a baby from one of our wards, Lyn. There'd be alarms sounding all over the place.'

She *knew* she was making a fool of herself. She should ask the taxi to turn round, and pay the cabbie extra for having to deal with an idiot. But she asked, 'What about Outpatients?'

Now there was steel in the calm voice. 'Outpatients. There's a thought—things have to be a bit more casual there. Lyn, we don't want to start a panic. Where are you?'

She gave him the name of the busy London street, and told him how slowly they were moving down it.

'Give me your phone number and I'll make a few enquiries and ring you back. How old was the baby?'

She gave him her number and said, 'I only had a quick look, but I think the baby was a neonate.'

'Narrows things down. I'll be in touch.'

He rang off. She watched the slow-moving traffic around her and wished heartily that she'd never started on this stupid adventure. It seemed like hours before her phone rang, but it was probably no more than five minutes.

'There's a baby missing from Outpatients. The mother was given a cup of tea by a nurse in scrubs, and told the baby had to be weighed. The mother was to sit there and take things easy. We're trying to control things here; we could do without this kind of trouble. Can you tell me exactly where you are? And can you see the number of the car with the baby?'

She could tell him both.

'Right, don't do anything until it's obvious you need to. Remember, you still might be quite wrong.'

'But how will…? Nothing can catch us here.'

'Just leave it to the police.'

She should have thought. A minute later there was the dull throb of a motorbike engine, and a policeman rode past on his gleaming machine. Two more threaded their way through the slow-moving traffic. Lyn watched anxiously, because this woman must be desperate. However, the policemen were clever. They stopped a van two vehicles in front of the little red car, and appeared to question the driver. The traffic had to stop. Then there was a policeman on each side of the red car, and a large arm reached in to take out the ignition key.

Lyn told the cabbie to wait, and then she was out of the taxi and running. The woman in the car was apparently not brazening out the situation, she knew there was no escape, was alternately screaming and sobbing, while the policeman restrained her gently. A vague recollection struck Lyn from a half-remembered psychiatry lecture that many women who stole children actually wanted to be caught.

Another policeman lifted an arm to stop Lyn. She grabbed for her hospital badge, and held it up like a talisman. 'I'm a doctor. I want to check the baby.'

'You're the one who phoned this in? Okay, ma'am.' She was allowed past.

Quickly she scrambled into the back of the car, and looked at the apparently happily sleeping child. It was a neonate, as she had thought before, perhaps three weeks old. She made a lightning examination, but there was nothing obviously wrong. She rang the hospital again, and got straight through to Ross McKinnon. 'I've got the baby, a little girl, she seems to be all right. Is there anything I should know?'

The voice was calm again. 'First, congratulations. No, there's nothing seriously wrong with the child. She was just in for injections and a check-up. Shortly there should be a police car arriving; it'll bring you back here with the baby. I suspect the mother is in a worse state than the child, so let's get them reunited.'

For some reason the scene in the middle of the crowded London street now reminded Lyn of a major surgical operation. The observers were kept well in the background and the chaos of policemen resolved itself into a set of men who knew exactly what they were doing and how best to do it. The traffic started to flow—slowly—around them. Somehow two police cars arrived, and the now quiet woman in the long coat was escorted firmly to one by a policewoman. 'Do we need an ambulance for the baby, ma'am?' Lyn was asked.

She shook her head. 'If you could drive me back to Lizzie's, please? Oh!' She foraged in her handbag, took out a twenty-pound note. 'Could you give this to the taxi driver and say thanks?'

'We'll be taking a statement from him anyway. Now, there's a car waiting for you if you're happy to carry the baby with you.'

Lyn decided to replace the baby in the cot he had trav-

elled in in the back of the red car. The little one would
be safer there. As Lyn lifted the cot out she noticed that
it was expensive, and brand-new. For a moment she wondered what personal tragedy she had touched on, what
could persuade a woman to steal a baby from another
woman. Surely the thief could share in the feelings of a
distraught mother? Lyn shrugged. She had learned early
that a doctor could not take on all the problems that her
work put forward.

She was settled in the back of the police car, with the
cot and baby again in the well behind the front seats. The
safest place. Then they were making remarkable speed
through the traffic back to the hospital. With a wry smile
she noticed how polite other drivers were when they saw
the police car behind them.

There was the crackle of the radio, and the driver was
announcing their arrival at the hospital. He was asked to
drive straight to the outpatients department, where they
would be expected.

A little welcoming committee was waiting by the pavement edge. There was a dark, intense-looking man in his
late thirties, a couple of nurses and an older man whose
cropped grey hair and general demeanour suggested the
army. Lyn opened the car door and slid the cot into the
waiting arms of the two nurses.

'I'm Edward Burrows, Outpatients Consultant,' the intense man said. 'What can you tell us?'

'I managed a quick examination and there doesn't appear to be anything wrong,' Lyn said concisely. 'And
since she got in the car I don't think the woman had a
chance to handle the baby.'

'Good.' He turned to the senior nurse. 'Sally, take
young Miss Charlotte here and reunite her with her
mother. Then in five minutes we'll give her a proper look-

ing over.' The two nurses disappeared with the cot as he turned back to Lyn. His rather bleak expression relaxed when he smiled, and she had to smile back, his joy was so obvious. 'It's Dr Webster, isn't it? Dr Webster, can you imagine the relief we're all feeling?'

'Possibly,' she said.

'We owe you, Dr Webster. If ever the outpatients department can do anything for you, just ask.'

'Careful. That kind of offer can get you into trouble. I could take advantage.'

'I very much doubt you will. Look, there's going to be no end of enquiries, meetings and paperwork about this, so I'd better practise medicine until it gets started. But once again, thanks.'

He strode into the department and she was left with the military-looking man who had just finished speaking to the police driver. 'Jock MacGregor, Head of Security at St Elizabeth's,' he introduced himself, and squeezed the hand she offered him. 'Rather an exciting beginning to your first day, Dr Webster. You spotted something that half a dozen of my staff missed.'

Lyn realised that the man took the theft of the baby personally, and liked him for it. 'It was sheer good luck on my part, Mr MacGregor. Now if it's possible I'd like to get to my new department. I'm late already. Will I have to make a statement? I'd much rather not, you know.'

'People will want to know what happened, Dr Webster. They'll think you're a heroine.'

'I took a ride in a taxi and used my mobile phone, that's all. I want to be a doctor, not a heroine. Can you keep my name out of things?'

For the first time Mr MacGregor smiled. 'We'll do what we can,' he said. 'Now, you'll find your way to your ward if you follow that corridor down to the main entrance hall.'

The main entrance to Lizzie's was through a glassed-in area. There was a mini-mall with a few busy shops: a flower and fruit shop with a grocery section, a toy and toiletries store, and a post office. Lyn passed through the hurrying crowds with an odd sense of unreality. She glanced at her watch, and couldn't believe the time. Only half an hour had passed since she'd approached those doors for the first time.

She remembered her apprehension, the nervousness that came with the beginning of any new job. And as she remembered it, the nerves returned. Good. The events of the past half-hour were now firmly behind her.

Now she too walked quickly, like nearly everyone else around her. Her long legs carried her towards the corridor marked 'Neurology Department'. Deftly she avoided a running child, then caught him as he stumbled. Children here often needed to run to keep up.

She had dressed with care—she always did. In a children's ward there was always a certain degree of informality. White coats and strict uniforms might reassure adults but they tended to frighten children. But Lyn always felt more confident if she also felt she was looking smart. She was wearing black suede flatties, dark trousers, and a grey silk sleeveless blouse. She knew there'd be a bright tabard available if she needed it, if she was going to do anything likely to be messy. Yesterday she'd had her dark hair dressed in its normal short cut. It had cost a small fortune but it made her feel good.

This was going to be the start of a new life. She remembered how almost exactly a year ago, in a different hospital, she had started on a ward as a completely new doctor, as a medical house officer. Then too she had thought she was starting a completely new life. She shivered. Things hadn't worked out as she had planned. This year things would be different.

Now she was outside the neurology department. From her bag she took the newly issued swipe card that let her through the locked doors. Then she walked to the doctors' room.

'Dr Webster—Lyn—welcome to the department. I do hope we can hang onto you! I gather Dr Burrows of Outpatients will offer you a place whenever you want one.'

She'd met him before, of course. Dr Birkinshaw had interviewed her for this post and showed her around the department at the same time. Only when she had left had she realised just how penetrating the interview had been. The questions had apparently risen from the children they'd been looking at. But they'd tested her knowledge to the full. His reputation—and that of the department—was worldwide. He was the reason she wanted to work in Lizzie's.

He was a short, wiry man, dressed in a dark suit with an immaculate white shirt and college tie. Dr Birkinshaw was a doctor of the old school; he liked to look the part.

'I want to work in Neurology,' she said as she shook his hand, 'perhaps even become a neurosurgeon. And I hope what happened this morning never happens to me again.'

Dr Birkinshaw nodded. 'Stealing a baby—a sign of the times, I'm afraid. When I first began medicine I never thought that I would see the day when we had to lock children's wards. Now, you must be shaken to a certain degree—I'll see if I can organise us some coffee. But first, this is Melissa Yates, my specialist registrar. You'll be spending much of your time with her.' He slipped out of the door.

'Pleased to meet you, Dr Webster,' Melissa said coolly. 'I hope you aren't going to excite us like this every morning.' Her handshake wasn't anything like as firm as Henry's had been. Lyn put her age at about thirty, she was carefully made-up, well dressed in what Lyn thought rather an unsuitably fussy dress and with long, artfully curled blonde hair.

'I've had enough excitement to last me the year,' Lyn agreed. Perhaps Melissa was one of those people who took some time to relax with newcomers. It was uncommon in medicine, for friendships were usually forged quickly.

'When I phoned earlier I spoke to someone else,' Lyn went on, 'a Dr...McKinnon?' She decided to tease Melissa a little. 'He had a lovely voice—very friendly.'

Now Melissa's voice was definitely glacial. 'Ross McKinnon. Our other specialist registrar. He had to leave.'

'I'm afraid Ross is spending much of his time at a neighbouring hospital,' Henry said, entering with a tray holding a cafetière and three cups. Lyn noticed that there was a cloth on the tray, and that they were cups and saucers, not the more usual mugs. Henry obviously didn't like slackness.

He went on, 'My esteemed colleague, Dr Johnson of Everton Heights Hospital, broke his leg in a skiing accident. There was no one in his own department who could safely take over his work while he convalesced, so very charitably I lent him Dr McKinnon. However, he is still my second specialist registrar.'

'It was charitable of Ross to volunteer,' Melissa put in. 'He's still doing most of his work here.'

Henry beamed at Lyn. 'A hard-working team is a happy team,' he said. 'I'm sure you agree?'

'I like work. That's why I'm here.'

'Good. Now, if you would like to sit down and drink your coffee, I'll just go through your duties this coming fortnight. I've got this schedule worked out...'

There was plenty for her to do, but not too much. Lyn felt that she'd learn here. She knew that she wanted to be a paediatric neurologist, and this was the best place in the country to become one.

'Now I have a clinic downstairs,' Henry said eventually, 'so I will leave Melissa to show you round and introduce you to the rest of the staff here. You can shadow her for the rest of the day. I hope you enjoy your stay with us.' With a courtly bow Henry left the room.

'We'll go and say hello to Sister first,' Melissa said. 'She can introduce you to the nursing staff.'

Lyn gulped the rest of her coffee, since Melissa apparently didn't intend to wait. However, she did intend to do her job, and as they moved down the corridor Lyn was given a clear description of where everything was.

There was a hum, and Melissa drew out her pager. She smiled as she saw the number on it. 'This will take a minute,' she said to Lyn. 'Why don't you go to Sister's office and introduce yourself? I'll pick you up there.'

Lyn did as she was told. She wondered who could have phoned Melissa, to bring so great a change in mood so quickly.

She tapped at Sister's door, and opened it when told to go in. Then she got the second big shock of the day. She recognised that matronly figure, that coal-black bobbed hair.

'Merry!' she squeaked.

Sister turned, her face at first blank, then creasing into

a smile. 'Lyn, my darling,' she cried, 'it's so good to see you.'

Lyn rushed over to hug her.

There was so much to say. Who would have believed that such good friends could have stayed out of touch for months? 'How's the baby?' Lyn started by asking. 'I heard you had a boy, but I didn't come...I mean...'

'Nathan is now five months old and my mother-in-law is looking after the baby in the day,' Merry said. 'Richard and I have bought a house—in fact, it's quite near...the flat where you used to live.'

'I still live there,' Lyn said. 'Merry, will you come round and bring the baby one evening this week? I'd love to see him.'

'And I'd love to come. We both would. I would have been before but it's just that things have been so hectic lately, having the baby, picking up this new job and also I heard that you were...working very hard.'

'I like working.'

'So are you all right now?'

'You get used to everything, Merry. And like I said, work helps. After the first couple of months...' Suddenly she was aware that the door had opened behind her, that Melissa had entered the room, and could be listening.

'Merry and I are old friends,' she told Melissa. For the moment she didn't care about the registrar's apparent coolness; she knew that her work here would be much, much easier with Merry as Sister. 'I was a medical house officer on her ward last year—she knew more than all us new little doctors, and she helped us no end. Then she left to have her baby and we lost touch.'

'We all know we're lucky in having Merry here,' Melissa said, and Lyn realised she meant it.

'Lyn's a good worker, Melissa,' Merry put in. 'I know my job will be easier with her on the ward.'

'You must tell me all about it later. Now, have you time to show us round the ward, Merry? Introduce Lyn to the rest of the staff?'

'It'll be my pleasure. Come on, Lyn.'

As the three of them moved out of the office Lyn caught a shrewd glance from Melissa. She wondered what the registrar had overheard, what she suspected. One thing was certain: Merry wouldn't tell her anything.

The neurology department consisted of two main wards, holding a variety of children from neonates to great fifteen-year-olds. Everyone seemed to be kept busy—there were plenty of parents and she saw a teacher giving a bed-ridden girl a lesson in geography. The rooms were bright, cheerful, the walls covered with pictures, many of them home-drawn. The fact that this was a hospital ward was played down.

Lyn knew, of course, that there would be other neurological patients, especially the post-operative ones, in the intensive therapy unit. Here they would be 'specialled': kept under twenty-four-hour surveillance by highly skilled nurses and technicians, and monitored by a variety of electronic devices.

'It's part of Henry's policy that our patients are always referred to by their names,' Melissa said. 'If he hears you referring to the Bell's palsy in bed five, then you're in trouble. Bed five is occupied by Katie Plant, who happens to have Bell's palsy. She's a person, not a disease.'

Lyn thought of other consultants she had met, and said forcefully, 'Good, I agree.' Melissa was obviously efficient. She introduced Lyn to each patient, chatted for a while and then gave Lyn a brief but adequate account of the child's condition. The tour was too soon over.

'Think you're going to enjoy working here?' Melissa asked at the end of the tour.

'Yes,' Lyn said with much determination. 'I am.'

CHAPTER TWO

THREE days later Lyn was firmly settled into the job. The work was absorbing, far more specialised than it had been in the general medical and surgical wards where she had done her house officer's job. When she had asked him, Henry had suggested three or four textbooks she should buy, and only when she pressed him did he admit that perhaps the book he had written might help her. 'It has gone through several editions,' he murmured. 'People appear to find it some use.'

'I'm afraid I shall have to ask you for a week off in a few months' time,' Lyn told him. 'I'll need to revise. I've already started studying for the Part One of the MRCS examination. I'd like to pass it first time.'

Henry peered at her. 'There's no shame in failing,' he told her. 'Some people take the exam dozens of times.'

'A lot pass it first time. It may be arrogant, but I want to be part of that number.'

'You may well be successful. I hope so. I approve of ambition if it is backed up by hard work.'

Now, no matter how tired she was, Lyn spent at least an hour every night reading up on the work she had done in the day and studying for the exam.

Her daily work was not too different from the work of an ordinary house officer. Much of it was not really medicine—it was organisation. She acted as the buffer between the patients, the parents, the laboratories, the theatres, the nurses, the GP's. There were a thousand forms, requisitions, orders, requests to be filled in. When Henry or one of his specialist registrars came on the ward, they expected all the details of a patient, all the examinations, bloods, X-rays, scans, to be immediately to hand. It was hard work, but she could see the point of it, and it was fun.

And there was always the clerking, the taking of the details of a new patient, the examination and the formation of her own diagnosis. Of course, she would never offer her opinion unless asked; the senior doctors diagnosed. But it was fun trying.

Amy Cross was just six weeks old. Her midwife and then her doctor had been troubled and she had been referred to Lizzie's for examination. As usual Lyn started by trying to make the mother relax. Henry had told her early on that the golden rule of paediatric examination was that the mother was always right until she was proved wrong. 'The mother has observed for all of a baby's life. Her intuition is to be trusted.'

Mrs Cross was a plainly dressed but obviously determined woman. Lyn felt that she was a good, concerned parent. 'I've had two already,' Mrs Cross said, 'both girls, and neither of them like Amy. Ever since she was born she's been—well, different.'

'Ever since she was born? Was she like the others when she was still in the womb?'

'Oh, yes. I could feel her kicking—kicking hard; I thought she was going to be a boy. And it wasn't a hard birth. But then...'

'How is she different?' Lyn queried.

'Well, the others were never still. Wriggling, crying, like babies are supposed to be. But Amy is just the opposite. She lies there and is no trouble at all, except that she's a poor feeder. And that's different from the other two. At first I thought I'd got a good baby at last, but then it started to worry me. I think I'd rather be disturbed a bit. And her head. I know baby's heads are supposed to be big, but…'

'Let's have a look, shall we?' Lyn said.

She knew the minute she saw baby Amy. The head was enlarged—almost the same circumference as the chest. When she looked at the skull she saw the dilated veins, the shiny skin, the bulging fontanelle. The separate bones of the skull should be knitting by now, but baby Amy's weren't. Carefully Lyn picked up the baby. Amy's eyes opened and Lyn saw what she had suspected; 'the sunset sign'. Amy couldn't look upwards.

'She's got water on the brain, hasn't she, Doctor?' Mrs Cross's voice sounded matter-of-fact, but Lyn could detect the terror behind it.

It was always difficult, trying to decide what to say to questions like this. The latest received opinion was that parents were entitled to know everything. However, some of them didn't want to know.

Choosing her words carefully, Lyn said, 'The signs do suggest that Amy has hydrocephalus—what you call water on the brain. We won't know for certain until we've sent her for a scan, but I should tell you that the diagnosis is likely to be positive.'

'Isn't there anything you can do?'

Once again she had to be careful. 'We can treat the hydrocephalus. What the surgeon will do is probably put in a shunt—that's a thin tube that will drain the excessive fluid out of the cranial cavity and lead it into the jugular vein.'

'And then she'll be all right?'

'Well, the tube will have to be replaced as Amy gets older and bigger. When she's eighteen months old, and perhaps a couple of times after that. But it's not a big operation.'

'So everything will be all right?'

Lyn thought Mrs Cross had had enough bad news for one day. About one third of children with hydrocephalus managed to live normal, happy lives. Some died, some were mentally impaired. 'We'll just have to see,' she said, 'but there is cause for hope.'

Mrs Cross started to weep, silently, recognising that Lyn was sparing her. 'Let me fetch you a coffee,' Lyn said.

Merry was in her room when Lyn walked in. 'I don't like it when I have to tell a mother that her child probably has hydrocephalus,' she said angrily.

'You'd have liked it even less a few years ago,' Merry said calmly. 'Then you would have said that the child had hydrocephalus and was certain to die. She's not certain to die now.'

Lyn stood silent for a minute. Then she went and hugged her friend. 'You're good for me, Merry,' she said.

She was in the doctors' room, busily writing up her notes, when the door opened behind her. 'And this must be Dr Lyn Webster, chaser of stolen babies,' she heard a voice say.

She recognised the voice at once, and it sounded even better than it had on the phone. That odd caressing tone was even more obvious. It wasn't a deep voice, but it was gentle and she felt that she'd pay more attention to a whisper from this man than to a shout from someone else.

She turned, desperately hoping that the rest of the man would live up to the voice, that he wouldn't be a disappointment.

He wasn't.

His eyes were blue, a deep, dark, intense blue. They fixed on her as if he knew what she was thinking, as if they could penetrate her very soul. And as he looked at her his eyes widened, in shock. He too didn't know what was happening. Just as she didn't. She felt spellbound by the blueness of those gorgeous, gorgeous eyes.

This had never happened to her before!

Both were silent. The little doctors' room with its table, magazines and easy chairs, seemed distant, as if the two of them were inhabiting a different dimension. All they could do was look at each other.

It was Lyn who spoke first. She managed to mutter something about being Dr Webster, he must be Dr McKinnon. He didn't reply. She was glad; she wasn't ready for a conversation yet.

She looked at the rest of him. He was big, shaggy, comfortable. Apart from the glorious eyes his face was pleasant, not too striking. His dark hair was a little longer than fashionable, his mouth wide and generous, showing good, even teeth. Somehow the face suggested he was everyone's friend, and she guessed that children would warm to him.

He was a sizeable man, with broad shoulders and big hands, but his size wasn't threatening. He was leaning comfortably against the wall, dressed casually in dark clothes. Just a pleasant-looking man, but those eyes... What woman wouldn't kill for eyes like that? She'd had nothing to do with men since...since then. Suddenly she was brought up short, shocked and a little frightened at the intensity of her own feelings. This wasn't her! With a desperate effort she collected herself.

'Your help was...' There was something wrong with her voice; it was too high. She stopped, coughed, tried again. 'Your help was much appreciated when I phoned,' she said. 'I was unsure, and even today I realise I could have been making a complete fool of myself.'

He seemed happy to think about this. 'You did what was exactly right. You suspected, but checked first. I wish all doctors would follow those two simple rules.'

Like her he was trying to find refuge in normality. Or did he not feel what had leaped between them, like some unearthed bolt of electricity? She couldn't believe it; she *knew* he had felt it. But for the moment they would play the game of being two new colleagues, getting to know each other, being suitably polite.

'How are you settling in?' he asked. 'Are you enjoying the work?'

'Very much so. There's a lot to learn. It's taking time but I'm enjoying learning.'

'I'm sure you are.'

Their conversation was stilted, but she didn't care. 'Anyway, I thought you were at Everton Heights Hospital, filling in for someone.' She was trying desperately to keep what she said normal, pretending that nothing had happened.

'I am. But I have a little flat here at the hospital where I live, and last night Melissa rang me with a query about Alice Tennant, one of her patients. I thought I'd drop in and have a look.'

'Alice Tennant,' Lyn said. 'Cheerful little girl, seven years old, got Guillain-Barré syndrome.'

Ross looked at her with renewed respect. 'You've only been in here three days and you know the patients. That's good. Tell me about this syndrome.'

'Inflammation of nerves, probably viral in origin,' Lyn said promptly. 'Alice started with just muscular pains in her thighs, the pains spread and then she started to get weaker. That's when she was referred to us. Now she's getting weaker, cranial nerve paralysis is setting in and she's having difficulty swallowing. I know Melissa thinks that the paralysis will get worse and now it's affecting her breathing…'

'I didn't know you'd arrived, Ross. One of the nurses told me you were on the ward.'

Melissa had entered, cool as ever. Lyn wondered if Ross had picked up on the tiny touch of sharpness in her voice. Then there was the make-up, applied with rather more than the usual care, and the dress which was far too expensive for a hospital ward.

'Just arrived. I was saying hello to our new recruit before coming to find you.'

'D'you want to see Alice? Lyn looked at her this morning but I'll get Merry and you can examine her yourself.' Melissa was determined to be businesslike.

Ross shook his head. 'No point in making Alice suffer unnecessarily. We'll hear what Lyn has to say; she's here to learn. Then we'll have a quick case conference. By the way, Melissa, are the legs still stiff?'

'I can certainly still feel them.' Obviously Melissa was pleased by the question. She turned to Lyn and said, 'Ross and I went away walking for the weekend—this man is a maniac for walking up mountains. London parks aren't good enough for him. Did you ever meet such people?'

'Yes,' said Lyn, 'I've met such people.'

But Melissa wasn't paying attention. 'What did we climb, Ross? That spikey thing? Tryffan?'

'Tryffan,' said Ross, getting the soft Welsh pronunciation exactly right.

'It's a good walk,' said Lyn, forgetting for the moment. 'Did you get up onto the Glyders, or go straight down again?'

Too late she realised she'd betrayed herself. There was

Melissa's cold glance, and awakening interest in Ross's eyes. 'Are you a mountain walker?' he asked.

'No, not really. I used to do a bit with my parents but it's all behind me now.' She needed a diversion. Reaching for her file on the table, she said, 'I've got Alice Tennant's notes here...'

Usually she managed to conceal it. But as she stretched out her arm across the table the inside of her elbow was revealed, and Ross, far more alert than his casual manner suggested, saw it.

'That's an interesting scar, Lyn. D'you mind telling me what caused it?'

Why should she mind? It was just an area of her life she didn't want Ross to know about—well, not yet. She could lie, of course—but she wouldn't. Trying to remain calm and indifferent, she said, 'As a matter of fact, it was a bit of emergency surgery when I was a child. I'd been bitten by a snake—a pit viper.'

She remembered it still. She'd been told to be careful, to avoid disturbing anything, not to go pushing through bushes. But her ball had rolled under some foliage, where she could see it, so she'd just reached in and...

'You don't cut into a bite by a snake! It spreads the venom even further!'

'I know that now. But the man in charge of our group didn't know, he panicked and did what he thought best. Fortunately there was a local anaesthetic that worked after a fashion. It was one of the things that made me want to be a doctor. My parents had been spending a day up country, but fortunately they came back early. The snake had struck in the vein so I was getting hypotensive. They gave me twenty millilitres of antivenin, and so I recovered. But my father wasn't much good at suturing.'

'Your parents! You're Jack and Jo Webster's daughter!'

Now it was out. 'Yes, I'm their daughter.'

Ross was obviously delighted. 'I read an article that said they had a daughter who was training to be a doctor. I thought it was a great idea. And you're a climber, too.'

Lyn was well aware that Melissa didn't at all like this turn in the conversation. Her face was frozen in a half-smile but her body language said that she was angry. Ross turned to her and said excitedly, 'This is great. Lyn's parents have been my heroes for years. You must have read their books, about their expeditions in South America, and Nepal, and bits of Africa.'

'I think I might have,' Melissa conceded frostily. 'Look, Ross, can we sort out this problem with Alice? I need to get on and I know you're needed back at Everton Heights.'

'Of course.' Now he was going to be fully professional. But before he reached for the notes he said, 'I want to talk to you more about your parents, Lyn. I'm hoping to spend a few years in South America myself, do some climbing, a bit of expedition work. I'm fed up with London, been here too long.'

'I've heard people say they feel that way,' Lyn said dully. 'It's never happened to me; I like London.' She didn't know what to feel, what to think. Not five minutes before she had met a man who had affected her more than any in her life, and now he was talking about an expedition to South America. There was only one thing to do—the thing she always did. She must seek refuge in work.

She found an unexpected ally in Melissa, who opened the notes on the table and said, 'Ross, we need to get on. Now, Alice is getting worse. She's getting increasingly distressed, having difficulty breathing. I'm wondering about an emergency tracheotomy and then perhaps mechanical ventilation.'

He read through the notes, and then sat at the table, frowning. 'I don't like cutting holes in little girls' throats unless it's absolutely necessary. You've got her on steroids?'

'Yes. They don't appear to be doing much good.'

'That's not unusual, but I suppose we have to try them. I would have said that her condition is about to improve. I'd like to avoid the tracheotomy. Come on, let's have a quick look at the patient. Coming, Lyn?'

His examination was quick but thorough. Alice liked the cheerful way he smiled at her, and tried to smile back, though her facial muscles were now partly paralysed. She was labouring for breath, her chest hardly expanding at all, and her lips were showing signs of cyanosis. Ross patted her on the shoulder and then led the little party away from her bed.

'It's distressing, I know, hearing her like that. But she's getting just enough oxygen. I wouldn't perform a tracheotomy just yet. Wait till the end of the day, see if there's any improvement. If there isn't, or if things have got worse, then operate.' He glanced at his watch. 'Now I really must move. Lyn, is there any chance of you arranging for me to meet your parents? There's an awful lot I'd like to ask them.'

'They're in Scotland at the moment,' Lyn said. 'But they'll be coming down south in a fortnight or so. They live near the Forest of Dean—when they're at home. Yes, I can arrange for you to meet them.'

'Good. I'll be in touch. Let me know about Alice, Melissa.' A last mouthful of the coffee they had poured for themselves and he was gone.

Lyn and Melissa sat in silence in the doctors' room,

each concerned with her own thoughts. Then Melissa said drily, 'You are doing well, aren't you, Lyn? Only met the man once and you're taking him home to meet your parents.'

Lyn ignored the barb. She said, 'He wants to lead an expedition, he wants to live in the wild end of South America, and he's a climber, never happy unless he's in the great outdoors. Melissa, that's exactly the kind of man I don't like, I don't want, and I wouldn't have under any circumstances.'

Melissa stared, open-mouthed at Lyn's angry outburst. Then she said, 'You mean that, don't you?'

'Yes,' said Lyn. 'I mean every word.'

She had a good afternoon. As ever, she found a respite in work. A neonate was admitted, and she had to take blood. It was hard but she found the tiny vein at the first attempt. She wanted to think about Ross McKinnon and the effect he had on her, but she couldn't while she worked. Besides, he wasn't the man for her.

Then, as she was walking through the mini-mall on her way out, she heard her name called. There was Ross walking towards her, tie loosened, coat over his shoulder, looking relaxed, casual and gorgeous in the late afternoon sun.

He smiled. 'Lyn, fancy meeting you here. This is a coincidence, isn't it?'

'Of course it is,' she said. 'A complete coincidence.'

'Ah. Do I detect an element of doubt? All right, I'll confess all, I rushed my afternoon surgeries just so I could be here to meet you. In fact, I wanted to take you for a drink. Have you got time?'

'I have an hour, but why do you want to take me for a drink? Can't we talk in the hospital?'

'I want to get to know all my junior staff. And especially the daughter of the Websters. Remember, people don't talk in the hospital, they communicate, or converse or put over their point of view. I want something a bit more casual.'

She looked at him dubiously. Perhaps she ought to start now, keeping him at a distance. That sudden flash of intimacy that had passed between them this morning was still in her mind. This man was dangerous to her. She couldn't, *wouldn't* let him get close to her. But he *was* one of her two specialist registrars, and she would learn a lot from him. She could feel herself weakening.

'All right, then. But just for an hour. I've work to do tonight.'

'In the neurology department everyone has work to do every night. But you can spare an hour.'

While they'd been talking he had manoeuvred her out of the great glass doors and they were now on the outside pavement. The sun struck down on them both, for it was a warm afternoon. He held her arm and escorted her across the busy main road as the pedestrian crossing beeped for them. 'You don't mind my taking your arm? More than a few women doctors would complain bitterly, either that I was harassing them or that I was treating them in a sexist fashion.'

She knew he was being light-hearted, but she answered his question seriously. 'No, I don't mind. I like a well-mannered man. Too many of my male colleagues think that treating me as an equal means treating me as one of the boys. That I don't want.'

'I could never mistake you for a boy, Dr Webster. How is young Alice, by the way?'

'There's a slight improvement. If it continues, then there'll be no need for a tracheotomy.'

'I'm glad about that.' He was conducting her, with an

ease that suggested long practice, through the maze of back streets and alleys that were hidden behind the great shops on the main road. Eventually they arrived at a pub, the Mayflower, situated on the corner of a tiny square. There were trees, seats beside them; it was warm enough to sit outside.

'This is just far enough from the hospital to ensure we don't meet any of the staff,' he said, leading her to a bench. 'I'm very fond of them, of course, but for a while I want you to myself. What may I get you to drink?'

They decided on a shandy each, for it was still quite early. When he had fetched the drinks they sat side by side, looking speculatively at each other. Her heart was racing, this man affected her so.

She had a sense of decisions being made, as if her destiny was bound up in what would be said over the next few minutes. She knew she was not just being silly. Around them were hurrying shoppers and office workers. There was the noise of distant conversations, traffic, the jukebox inside the pub. But she was in her own little universe, insulated from all around her. She knew he felt the same. He was looking at her, puzzled, as if not quite sure how to begin.

'It must be wonderful having parents like Jack and Jo Webster,' he said eventually. 'Are you an only child?'

'Yes, I'm an only child. And I love my parents dearly, but I'm nothing like either of them.'

'What are you like?'

'I'm a hard-working junior doctor, happy to live in London, who has just landed the job she wants. I love neurology and I want to learn all about it.' She wanted to deflect his enquiries as long as possible. 'What about you? What are you like?'

He shrugged. 'I'm a hard-working senior doctor. I enjoy the work no end and I know it's time I started looking round for a consultancy. But I don't want to yet. Once you're a consultant you're expected to stay in the same place for years, if not for ever. I don't want that.'

'You can miss the boat,' she told him. 'There's only a few years when you can look for the exact right job. Every year there are more bright people coming up underneath. You might have to stay as a registrar, floating round from one post to another.' She stopped for a moment and then added, 'I think that would be a pity.'

He frowned. 'I'm not going to live my life sniffing round after promotion. If I'm worth it, then there should always be a job for me.'

In one way she didn't really want to know. She suspected that what he would tell her would drive a wedge deep between them. Perhaps it would be best to know before they got—well, too close. So she asked, 'What were you saying about working in South America?'

He was instantly enthusiastic, so enthusiastic that he didn't notice that his enthusiasm wasn't shared. 'There's an American charity called AndesAid. They build and supply hospitals in the more remote parts of the South American highlands. The ultimate aim, of course, is to make the hospitals self-supporting, with their own native trained staff, but this takes some years to set up. I met one of the high-ups of the charity when I was on a climbing expedition last year in Kenya, and he said there was a new hospital being set up in Peru, there could be a job for me there. The work would be interesting, and there would be chance to do more climbing—some of the peaks there haven't yet been visited by Europeans. He told me that he'd been attacked by a condor when he was on a peak there; imagine that—a bird with a ten-foot wingspan! Wouldn't that be something?'

Lyn shivered. She had met this kind of enthusiasm before, and she didn't like it. It could be dangerous. 'I'd rather be an SR or a consultant in London,' she said.

He looked at her, amazed. 'I thought the idea would really grip you. I thought we were soul mates.'

She had to tell him, clearly and finally. 'No. I've seen enough of the rough side of South America to last me a lifetime.'

'But…'

'I'm a city girl. I'm quite happy to stay in London for the rest of my life, only leaving when I can be sure of a warm bed in a comfortable hotel.'

'Hmm.' She could tell he was having difficulty in coming to terms with this, but he went on, 'I've read your parents' book about travelling the highlands of Peru. I was hoping to meet them, they might be able to give me a couple of ideas about the place.'

'I'm sure they'd love to meet and talk to you,' she told him, and knew that it was true. 'I'll set it up as soon as they're home again; we can go down for the day.'

'But you're not an outdoors girl yourself?'

'Not any more.' Gloomily she decided that she might as well tell him the rest of her doubts. 'And I think your skills would be wasted in the highlands of Peru. I've been there. South America needs a large number of locally recruited "village doctors", not a handful of highly trained European specialist like yourself.'

'So the poor peasants aren't entitled to the best care?' For the first time since she'd met him, she thought she detected a touch of bad temper.

'That's not the point. You're a highly skilled paediatric neurologist, you see patients referred to you from all over the country, and even all over the world. To do your job properly you need a state-of-the-art hospital, with specialist operating theatres, laboratories, carefully trained nurses and ancillary staff. In the highlands of Peru you'd have none of that. No matter what knowledge you had, you'd be little better than a doctor fresh out of college.'

'I think more than just a little better,' he suggested. 'I think I have skills in diagnosis that take quite some years to develop.'

She nodded, to acknowledge that this was true. 'But most of your work on Peru would be taken up with the simpler kinds of medicine. Lord knows, there's a need for it and I'm sure it could be very satisfying. But your unique skills are needed here. They would not—they could not— be used in Peru.'

'You argue well, young Dr Webster,' he said with a sudden smile, and she wondered what she was doing, possibly antagonising this man. When he smiled, and those blue eyes stared straight at her, she would agree to whatever he suggested. But...

'No matter what I say, you're still going to go, aren't you?' she asked.

'Probably. I agree with much of what you say. But I want—if only for a few years—to get out of England. I need to wander. I'm sure your parents would sympathise—I'm surprised you don't.'

She sighed. 'My parents would sympathise, all right. I'll certainly arrange for you to meet them, you'll get on together so well.'

'What if it's the daughter I want to get on with?'

'I'm looking forward to working with you,' she said demurely. 'I hope to learn a lot.'

'I hope to teach you a lot,' he replied, and she blushed as she saw his grin. He went on, 'We only have time for an hour now, and that's nearly over. But I want to see more of you, out of the hospital. Could we have dinner together some time this week?'

She wanted so much to say yes. But she knew it could only ultimately lead to disaster. Better a small pain now than absolute heartache in time. 'I don't think it's a good idea,' she said. 'Perhaps we should keep things between us largely professional.'

He frowned. 'Save me making a fool of myself. Are you seeing anyone now—are you in any kind of relationship?'

It would be so easy to lie. She suspected that he was an honourable man, and if she said that yes, she was in love, she felt that he would bother her no more. But she couldn't deceive him that way. 'No. As they say, I'm footloose and fancy free. All I want to do is study.'

'You don't seem very footloose to me,' he said sourly. 'Lyn, I felt that something happened between us this morning. I don't know what it was, because it's never happened to me in my life before. Are you telling me that you didn't feel the same?'

Once again, the easiest thing to do would be to lie, and once again she couldn't do so. She had never backed down from a fight, a hard decision. 'I felt it,' she agreed. 'It was just hormones, Ross, we'll both get over it.'

'Hormones! And I thought you might be a romantic young woman! Anyway, what's wrong with doing what our hormones suggest? As a doctor you should know that they were given us with a very definite purpose.'

'As a doctor you should know that the brain controls the actions of the hormones. And on this occasion my brain tells me not to do what my feelings might want me to. Sorry, Ross.'

She had wondered if he might be angered by such a firm refusal. But instead there was a thoughtful gleam in his blue eyes. 'Why do I get the feeling that I'm not getting all the story?' He glanced at his watch. 'Our hour's up, Lyn. I've got a meeting in fifteen minutes, I must go.'

She rose as he did. 'I've enjoyed our talk. I think we've settled a couple of things.'

'I've enjoyed talking to you, too. We might have settled some things but we've also raised one or two more questions. Shall I walk you back to the hospital?'

'No, I'll take a taxi from here.' Providentially, as she spoke one came down the street towards them and she waved it down. He held the door for her as she climbed in. 'Thanks for a pleasant drink, Ross.'

'Till the next time,' he said, and shut the door. She wondered what he meant by that.

It was only a short journey back to her flat, which was a good thing. She needed to start work on something, not be alone with her thoughts. Ross was an attractive man, a *very* attractive man. But he wasn't her sort. She couldn't go out with someone like Ross. Never again.

CHAPTER THREE

'YOU'VE decorated,' Merry said. 'Lyn, it's lovely.' She indicated the carry-cot she was swinging easily in one hand. 'Young master here is still asleep, so let's park him somewhere and you can show me round properly.'

'We'll put him on the bed,' Lyn said.

It was Thursday evening, straight after work. Merry had a very tight schedule, but she could get away for a while after picking up her baby, and she wanted to see Lyn in her flat again.

They walked through the hall, with its muted grey walls and white stencils, into the bedroom. Merry carefully placed the carry-cot on the bed. At times it still looked odd to Lyn, the single bed in the alcove that had once held a double, but now she was used to it.

She walked to the window to draw the curtains, and Merry joined her, to look out. This was the reason Lyn had first picked the flat. It was the first floor of a house, skilfully converted into two. The bedroom, and the living room next door, looked out over a tiny park, and then the ground dropped away so they could see the towers and spires of the City of London in the distance. Lyn never tired of the view. She had spent many hours just staring, wondering at the lives of the countless thousands below her. It had been comforting, in a strange way. It had made her own problems seem in proportion.

'I'm surprised you didn't move,' Merry said directly.

Lyn waved at the view. 'I didn't want to leave this. Moving would have seemed like running, so I stayed. But everything had to be exactly as I wanted it, so I redecorated this summer. Mum and Dad wanted me to fly out to go on a trip with them, but I wanted to get my life in order.'

They moved into the living room, and Merry smiled at the essentially feminine décor. 'This is lovely,' she said. 'How did you get the contrasting curtains and carpet? And those pictures of flowers, they fit in so well. As I remember, the place was a bit of a hodgepodge. All bits and pieces. Now it's all of a piece.'

'It all took some finding but it was worth it. I wanted a place that was completely mine, that reflected no one's life but mine. And now I think I've got it. Come and look in the kitchen.'

They walked into the hall again. 'There used to be another bedroom there,' Merry said, 'quite a big one. Have you decorated that too?'

'Try the door,' Lyn said.

Merry did so, then turned, surprised. 'It's locked,' she said.

'It's full of the furniture and things from before. Stuff I can't yet bear to give away.'

'Full of memories,' Merry said.

'If you like. But they'll go soon. I've started a new life.'

From the bedroom came a little wail. 'Her master's voice,' Merry said. 'D'you mind if I feed him, Lyn?'

'Bring him into the living room and I'll fetch us a biscuit and a cup of tea. Then we can have a talk.'

Merry had said she wouldn't stay for a full meal, for her husband was a GP and they liked to have dinner together at about seven. So they just had tea, and talked as Merry breast-fed the baby. Lyn peered at the urgently sucking infant. There was something inexpressibly touching about the fervour with which a baby suckled.

'You should have a baby.' Merry chuckled. 'It's nothing like what I expected. For years I lectured new mums on having babies, and when I had one I realised I hadn't known what I was talking about.'

'I want to in time,' Lyn said, 'but first I've got other plans. Now, come on, gossip. Tell me about the other members of the department. What's Henry really like?'

'Ah, Henry. He's got a clear mind, he knows his stuff, he can be a bit detached but he's really very human. I think he preferred life as it was in the fifties, when doctors were God and everyone else had to know it. Life was simpler for him then. But he's adapted and now we all can call him Henry.'

'That seems exact,' Lyn agreed, 'and I *am* learning from him. He's a brilliant neurologist.'

'Why did you opt for neurology?' Merry asked. 'As I remember you were thinking about orthopaedics for a while. Together with—'

'I just wanted a change,' Lyn interrupted. 'And neurology really is fascinating. Now what about Melissa? She's been helpful enough, but she seems a bit cool.'

'Comes from an old family of doctors,' Merry said, lifting Nathan and expertly rubbing his back. 'Her father is Sir Sidney Yates, you know, the cardiologist, and she's got a younger brother who's some kind of doctor too. She certainly knows her stuff.' Baby burped. 'There's a good boy,' Merry crooned, then giggled. 'I think Melissa is a bit upset after her weekend with Ross.'

'I know they were walking in Wales. Did they go away together—you know, as in a weekend away?' Lyn didn't feel this was like Ross. Surely he wouldn't have been so attentive to her, just a couple of days after a weekend with Melissa? Certainly she hoped not.

Melissa giggled again. 'I don't think so. I suspect Melissa wouldn't have minded—she would have quite liked a weekend with Ross in some posh hotel. Last week I heard her on the phone to him, practically forcing him to take her away. Said that Henry was on call all weekend, and they didn't spend enough time together out of the department. So Ross invited her. You know he's a big outdoor type, like...you used to be. Well, she wanted to go with him, so he took her.'

'Go on,' Lyn said with a small smile. She already suspected the end of this story.

'Ross took her to a North Wales Climbing Club hut, to meet a few of his pals. That was it, a hut. Melissa had to sleep in a dormitory with the other girls. She had to wash in cold water, and use a chemical toilet. And Melissa had to pretend to enjoy it, and the joke is, Ross thought she did. He couldn't imagine anyone *not* enjoying that kind of experience.'

'I know the kind of man you mean,' Lyn said. 'So now tell me about Ross. He took me for a drink, you know— said he wanted to get to know new members of staff.'

Merry looked at her shrewdly. 'He does that, he took me too. The first thing to know about Ross is that he does a lot of Henry's work. They're partners rather than consultant and SR. Apart from that I think I'll leave you to make up your own mind about Ross. Like I said, he's a big outdoors type, rather like you used to be—though you're not now.'

'I've met these big outdoors types before,' said Lyn. 'They're full of charm and they cause no end of trouble. Now tell me about working when you have a baby at home...'

It was a short but very pleasant visit. Lyn agreed to come round for tea soon, so she could have a chat with Joe, Merry's husband. Then she frowned when Merry had left. It was too long since she'd had a visitor in her flat. She mustn't turn into a hermit. She'd ring one or two of her other old friends. Quite soon.

Slightly dissatisfied with her life, Lyn finished her tea, picked up the evening paper and idly scanned through the entertainments section. Something caught her attention. On Saturday night there was a concert she would really like to attend. It was by a singer who had had a period of fame in the sixties, had then followed the familiar route of drugs, failure and a disastrous personal life. But now, in her mid-fifties, had come a new career. She had started to sing again. Her voice was hoarse, sad, knowing, hinting at the experiences of the past thirty years. Lyn rang the box office at once.

'Sorry, we're booked up,' the clerk said. 'But if you can give me a daytime telephone number and a credit card number, I'll ring you if we get any returns.' There was a chance. Lyn gave the ward number, and hoped she'd be lucky.

In fact, she was. When she came back to the doctors' room next morning there was a note for her. Her ticket for the concert would be waiting for her at the box office. Good. She was starting to get out at last.

'A young girl, Fatima bin Hameed has just been sent up from A and E,' Merry said. 'Suspected skull fracture and complications. She speaks no English, but her uncle who does is with her.'

There was something about Merry's tone that made Lyn look up. 'Come on,' she said, 'what is it?'

'He's arrogant, thinks because he's rich that he owns everybody. But the poor girl's got to be clerked.'

'It's part of the job.' Often dealing with parents was painful, and occasionally it was downright unpleasant. But for a paediatrician it was part of the job.

Lyn took a junior nurse and walked to the little side ward where Fatima was lying. She was a small dark child, about five years old, with big luminous eyes. Lyn twitched. She thought one of the pupils was bigger than the other. The child was obviously terrified.

A man in western clothes had his back to Fatima, and was staring out of the window. Lyn said, 'Mr bin Hameed? I am Dr Webster.' The man turned slowly, and after a pause he took Lyn's outstretched hand.

'This is my niece Fatima,' he said. 'Earlier today I sent for the doctor, and he requested that we come here at once. I think it is nothing.'

'Tell me what happened,' Lyn said evenly.

The man shrugged. 'Really, I do not know. Her nurse said that yesterday Fatima slipped while playing, and hit her head against the corner of the table.'

'Was she knocked unconscious?'

'Possibly. Certainly she has slept much since it happened.'

'What kind of nurse was she with? A medical nurse?'

'I do not know. Just someone sent by the agency.' Mr bin Hameed was getting restless. 'This is most inconvenient. I am not married, and my brother left this child with me. If I may leave her to your care now?'

'No,' said Lyn. 'We may need your signature giving permission for an operation.'

'Operation! For a headache?'

Already Lyn suspected what was wrong, but she had to be systematic. Fatima had drifted off to sleep, so gently she shook her awake. With the nurse's help Lyn rolled back the bedclothes and checked that there were no other signs of trauma, no other injuries. Then the vital signs—pulse, breathing, blood pressure. She wanted to assess Fatima on the Glasgow coma scale, giving her scores on eye opening, verbal response and motor response. Fatima didn't do too well.

'Ask her to lift her legs slightly,' Lyn told the uncle. 'And now her arms.' After this there was little doubt. Fatima could only lift one side. She was suffering from hemiplegia—her left side was paralysed.

Lyn took a sample of blood, and sent it down to be matched. Then she made arrangements for Fatima to have a CCT scan—a cranial computerised tomography scan. The results would take about an hour. The she bleeped Melissa, who was on duty.

'Five-year-old child,' she said. 'I suspect an acute sub-dural haematoma. I think her condition is worsening.'

'You've sent her for a CCT?'

'Of course,' said Lyn, slightly nettled.

'I'm on my way down. See if you can organise a theatre and an anaesthetist. Do the parents want to speak to me?'

'It's an uncle. And I don't think he wants to speak to anyone.'

'Like that, is it? Well, get his signature anyway.'

'Melissa,' Lyn asked, 'can I come and watch?'

There was a pause, then she answered, 'Why not? If you're sure you're not needed on the ward.'

Melissa came down, checked Lyn's findings and the two of them looked at the CCT results together. There had been a linear fracture of the skull—it hadn't shown clearly on the initial X-ray. Both of them could clearly see where blood and fluid had drained into the space between the brain and the dura, the membrane that contained the brain. This was exerting pressure on the brain. 'Better get that drained,' said Melissa.

Lyn managed to get a signature from the uncle, but when she tried to explain what they were going to do, and the possible, if unlikely dangers, he just didn't want to know. 'I leave her in your hands,' he said.

'Aren't you going to wait till the operation is finished?' asked Lyn, amazed.

'I will phone tomorrow morning. I am a busy man.'

Fatima was prepped, and her hair shaved, as Lyn and Melissa scrubbed up. Then they were in the theatre. 'I don't think we need a full craniotomy,' Melissa said, critically studying the CCT. 'A burr hole should do.'

Lyn watched as Melissa cut through to the skull, and her nerves twitched just a bit as the drill started to grind into the white bone. Blood gushed out, with Melissa looking on approvingly. Then the hole was sealed, and a probe to measure the pressure left protruding.

'All we can do now is wait and hope,' Melissa said as they stripped off the theatre greens and threw them down the chute. 'But I think we caught it before the pressure on the brain got too serious. I'll be down to see her tomorrow.'

Lyn walked slowly back to the ward. Soon Fatima would wake, and be alone in a foreign environment, with no one to talk to, no friendly face to comfort her. That uncle was a pig!

'Who's the Arabic translator?' she asked Merry. Lizzie's treated many foreign children, most of whom could speak no English. There was a register of translators—either people who worked in the hospital, or others outside who could be called on.

'There's a staff nurse in orthopaedics,' Merry said. 'She might be on duty now.'

This was a situation in which other wards were usually willing to lend staff if they could. Lyn arranged for the nurse to come onto the ward next morning for half an hour. When Fatima woke there would be at least one person who could talk to her.

Lyn was looking forward to Saturday night. There was no problem about going out on her own, for she was used to her own company and knew she'd enjoy herself. In fact she did phone a couple of old friends, but both of them were busy over the weekend, going out with long-standing partners. Lyn was a little shaken to see how life was passing her by.

Just because she was going on her own there was no reason for not making an occasion of the night. She loved dressing up, so she treated herself to a long, luxurious bath, had a suitably self-indulgent period at her dressing table, then put on a burgundy silk dress she had bought only a couple of weeks before, and not yet worn. She phoned for a taxi, and threw an ivory-coloured wrap round her shoulders. Might as well do things in style.

She picked up her ticket, bought a glossy programme, and for a while enjoyed herself mingling with the other well-dressed people in the foyer. Then she went to take her place early. It was an expensive seat, so there would be plenty of leg room.

She found her place, and discovered she was next to a large man in a dinner jacket, who had his back to her. She sat down. The man turned and she looked at him in disbelief. 'Good evening, Lyn,' said Ross. He placed something in her lap. 'Here, just to be conventional I've bought you a box of chocolates.'

She couldn't keep the rage out of her voice. 'What are you doing here?'

'I came to hear the concert. I'm very fond of this singer.'

'I suppose it's a coincidence that you're sitting next to me?'

He was entirely unapologetic. 'Not at all. I took the call on the ward when the box office rang. The booking clerk said there were two seats and you wanted one. I didn't presume to order for you, but I took the other for myself.'

'So why didn't you tell me?'

'You might have objected,' he said urbanely. 'This way I am certain of your company, at least for the first half of the programme.'

'You're chasing me!'

'Not at all. I'm just discovering we have interests in common. I like this singer too, I have all her CDs. And after we have enjoyed the music together I will take you to supper and you can tell me why you are trying to keep me at a distance.'

'Have supper with you! I'd rather…?'

'Shh! We're starting.'

He was right: the lights were going down; the hum of voices decreased; in the pit the orchestra started to play quietly. The magic of the evening was beginning. A single spotlight flashed onto the stage, and into it walked a slight figure, pale-faced, dark-haired. There was applause, much applause, and then the figure began to sing.

She was one of the few singers who took care that every word could be heard. This was important, for the words were as necessary as the music. Lyn gave herself to the mood created, of melancholy, of lost love, of the transience of memory. It was just the kind of music she needed. Occasionally she stole glances at Ross, and he seemed just as rapt as she was.

By the interval she was in an entirely different mood,

inclined to forgive him, and so she accepted his invitation
to go for a drink. He told her he had ordered for them
both in advance, hoping that she would approve of his
choice.

She sipped the small glass he offered her. 'Malt
whisky?'

'The Laphroaigh. The finest malt there is. I never knew
a climber who didn't like it.'

'I told you, I'm not a climber.' But she enjoyed the
drink anyway, the smoky warmth relaxing her.

She was aware of other people looking at them, and
guessed it was because Ross looked singularly well in his
dinner jacket. There was a contrast between the formality
of his well-cut black and white clothing and his general
outdoor look. She even caught a couple of envious looks
from other women, and felt a faint proprietary pride. She
was glad she had put on her expensive burgundy dress.

'I'm glad to be spending the evening with you,' he said
affably. 'Aren't you glad to be spending it with me?'

'Perhaps not. Perhaps I just don't fancy you,' she said.

'But you do. We both know that. I've never felt anything like this before, Lyn, and that is the truth. You told
me you were not seeing anyone else, so why shouldn't
you be with me?'

She paused before answering, knowing that she was
going to shock him. Well, he had pursued her. She had
intended to keep her past life to herself, not to get involved with anyone. He had asked why he shouldn't be
with her, so she would tell him.

Calmly, she said, 'One reason is perhaps because my
fiancé, the man I was going to marry at the end of this
month, has only been dead for eight months.'

He *was* shocked. 'I didn't know that,' he said quietly.
'I'm sorry I presumed. Please accept my apologies.'

'That's all right,' she said. 'I'll go to supper with you anyway.'

If anything the second half of the concert was better than the first. There were three encores before the audience would finally leave. But eventually they all spilled out of the concert hall, and Ross and Lyn walked along the Embankment. The evening was still warm.

'I like the lights on the darkness of the river,' Ross said. 'It makes me think of travelling to foreign cities. Romantic places. All rivers do that, I suppose.'

'If you'd already met my parents,' she told him, 'they'd agree with you at once. They'd say you have itchy feet like they have.'

'Ah. Itchy feet. Do you have itchy feet, Lyn?'

'No,' she told him firmly. 'And if they do itch, they itch to be in a pair of slippers, and by my own fire.'

'I see. I've got an itchy hand at the moment. It wants to hold yours.'

She reached her hand out to him. 'Everyone needs a little comfort sometimes,' she told him. 'I learned that.'

The restaurant was over a riverside pub. He told her he had booked in advance but said that he might have to cancel. 'It looks very nice,' she said, glancing up at the magnificent Victorian brick decorations, 'but I'm afraid I'm not tremendously hungry.'

'Neither am I. We're not going to have a full-sized meal, just an after-concert supper with a bottle of wine. We can leave the choice to Luke if you like.'

He led her into the building. Downstairs the bars were heaving, but upstairs, where the restaurant was, was much quieter. They were met by a *maître d'hôtel*, who greeted Ross by name.

'This is Lyn Webster, Luke—she's Jack and Jo Webster's daughter.'

Luke, a fit, burly man in his early forties who didn't seem at all like a typical hotelier, looked at her with interest. 'Very pleased to meet you, Miss Webster. If your parents would care to come to dinner one evening, I could assure them a good meal.'

'That's very kind of you. I'll be sure to tell them.'

They were led to a table that overlooked the river, and, looking round, she decided it was the best in the house. 'Do you always get service like this?' she whispered to Ross.

'Only from Luke. I met him some years ago in Thailand. He claimed he was researching Thai cooking, but he didn't see much cooking when he was with me. We decided to go up country together, and it was an...experience.'

'I might have guessed,' she said.

'As I said before, if you like, we can leave the choice of menu to him. But what kind of wine would you like? Should we have champagne?'

'I'm afraid I'm going to be rather unfeminine. I like red wine—strong, with lots of oak. Spanish rather than French.'

'Luke's going to approve of you,' he said with a grin. 'A Rioja it shall be.'

The wine was just as she liked it, so dark as to be nearly black, with a rich earthy taste and the faint suggestion of flowers. 'This is *good*!' she exclaimed.

Luke, who had just poured, nodded judiciously. 'Yes,' he said, 'it is good.'

The meal he provided was more than good. They had grilled breast of duck with a fruit compote, a slightly bitter leaf salad and hot rolls. She found she had more appetite than she had thought. Afterwards there was ice cream with a ginger sauce.

'That was marvellous,' she sighed as their plates were removed. 'I don't think I've ever had a meal quite like it.'

'You must let me bring you again. I come quite regularly.' He leaned over to refill her glass. 'We have half the wine left. Time to sit and talk.'

'Yes. Time to sit and talk.' It was months since she'd really talked to anyone; perhaps it would help her. 'What d'you want to talk about?'

'I want to know about you. All about you.'

She paused a moment, her eyes searching the dark river passing below, and then she said, 'You need to start by understanding my parents. I'm an only child. My parents loved me dearly, they still do. We're a loving family. But my parents loved travelling too, and they saw no good reason why they should stop travelling just because they had a young daughter in tow. They were constantly on the move to somewhere new, exploring, writing. D'you know I've visited over half the countries there are in the world?'

'But you became a doctor. To get into medical school you must have studied somewhere.'

'When I was fifteen my grandmother put her foot down. She said I was to stay at home, study constantly instead of whenever it was convenient. So I stayed with her in term time and worked at the local school. My parents were amazed when I said that was what I wanted to do—they had thought I was perfectly happy wandering with them.'

'And you weren't?'

'I was just learning that there was more to life than I had known so far. When I was seventeen I flew out to the north of Canada to stay at a camp with my parents. There were a lot of American students there, and they voted me the student they'd most like to be marooned on a desert island with. Not because I was attractive, but because I could hunt, fish and make a shelter. I didn't take this as the compliment they intended it to be.'

She waved at the scene around them, the elegant room, the well-dressed diners, the attentive staff. 'This is how I like to dine, not squatting under a bush trying to fry lumps of meat on a smoking fire.'

He grinned. 'If you've tried one, then you certainly appreciate the other. Surely there's a place for both?'

'Possibly. But I've had plenty of the one and I want to catch up on the other.'

'I see.' He looked at her thoughtfully. 'You're moving towards telling me something that's making you uncomfortable, aren't you? Are you sure you want to now? I can wait, you know.'

Once again she was surprised by his ability to gauge her mood. He seemed to know what she was feeling before she did herself. Under that hard exterior was a surprising subtlety.

'No, you've asked me, so now I want you to know exactly how I feel. Then there can be no mistakes. You will have to take me as I am.'

'It sounds as if you think that will be hard.'

'For you it might be,' she told him.

'So tell me about your dead fiancé. That's the heart of the matter, isn't it?'

'Yes. That's the heart of the matter.' She sat in silence for a minute, tasting her wine, running her newly dampened tongue over her lips. Patiently, he waited for her to begin.

She said, 'The Freudians would have a field day with me. They'd say I wanted to marry a replica of my father.

I got engaged to a doctor called Gavin Bell. He was a couple of years older than me. And he was never at home. He was constantly away on some pointless expedition or other, walking across Greenland or canoeing up to the source of the Amazon, or climbing peaks that no one had ever climbed before. Climbing was what he liked best. Anyway, he went with a group into some unexplored bit of Borneo, sneaked off climbing on his own, fell off a cliff—apparently quite a little cliff—and died.'

'I remember it being reported,' Ross said quietly. 'Weren't there two brothers?'

'Yes. Sometimes I think Gavin was closer to Doug than he was to me. Doug used to just turn up at the flat I shared with Gavin, and sleep in the loft.'

She knew her voice had become shaky, and with an effort she controlled it. 'Anyway, now I'm making a statement. For me, no more daring men. I want nothing to do with men who climb mountains, sail the Atlantic in a canoe or ski across Antarctica. I want two-point-four children, a house in the suburbs and a husband who comes home every night. I don't care if he works late, so long as he comes home at some time. Any man who deliberately risks his life is out!'

'I've heard that central London is more dangerous than any mountain range,' he pointed out.

'It might be. But you don't throw yourself in front of the traffic deliberately.' Suddenly her voice was shaking again, and quietly Ross offered her his handkerchief. Out of the corner of her eye she saw Luke moving towards their table, and to her surprise he placed a glass of iced water in front of her then moved swiftly away. That was kind of him, she thought.

She took a draught of the water, and wiped her eyes. 'Sorry,' she said. 'I'm not usually so emotional.'

'You're a doctor, you should know that there's nothing wrong with emotions, especially grief. Did you have any counselling when it happened?'

'I know all about grief management, and I know all the stages because I've been to the lectures. Let me tell you, they don't do much good. No, I didn't have counselling, I just lost myself in work. I was well into my first house officer's job, so I threw myself into that.'

'How many people have you talked to about it?'

'As few as possible,' she said. 'Merry was Ward Sister, and she helped me quite a bit, but mostly I just got on with my work. Now, I've told you all about my recent past—now I want to know about you.'

'Certainly I'll tell you all about me. But right now you don't want me to, do you? Talking to me has brought back memories—you're in pain.'

Now the tears were running down her face. 'All I need to do is work,' she said. 'It's easy to forget when you work.'

He nodded. 'That's one way. Perhaps we'd better get you home. I'll ask Luke to get us a taxi.'

It seemed no time at all before they were drawing up outside her flat. He paid off the taxi, and walked with her to the door. She wondered if he would want to come in; yet, like him though she did, she didn't want him in her home tonight. With his apparent insight to her feelings, he recognised this.

In the cover of her porch he kissed her gently, like a brother rather than a lover. 'I've enjoyed tonight,' he said. 'The concert and the meal were both memorable, and if I've made you suffer by scratching over old wounds, then I hope in time you'll think it worthwhile.'

'I told you what I did to warn you off,' she said.

'I'm afraid it will take more than that. By the way, if

I had a vote, I'd vote for you as the girl I would most like to be marooned with on a desert island.'

She giggled. 'That's a compliment I shall treasure.'

'What are you doing tomorrow?'

Well, she wasn't going to see him. She needed time to think. 'Working,' she said. 'I've got a lot of reading up to do, notes to take.'

Once again, uncannily he knew what she was thinking. 'I won't push you, I think you need more time to mourn,' he said. 'Just one thing, Lyn. I think there could be something between us. In fact, I know there already is. I don't want to lose it.'

'I need time,' she said uneasily.

CHAPTER FOUR

'WIND-DOW,' said Lyn, pointing. 'Wind-dow.'

Lyn pointed to the door. 'Dower,' Fatima said hesitantly.

'You're coming on, Fatima,' Lyn said cheerfully. 'You'll soon be speaking English as well as most in this ward. Here, have a drink.'

'Orange,' said Fatima.

The uncle had phoned, but not visited again. Apparently he was too busy. There was a limit to the amount of time the staff nurse from Orthopaedics could come over. So Lyn had started to visit the little girl, to stop for a chat even though she knew Fatima didn't understand a single word. She thought—she hoped—that it would help.

'There's a sparkle in your eyes,' Merry said to her when they sat in her office, having a comfortable coffee, mid-Monday morning. 'You've been up to something. Tell me all about it.'

Lyn was surprised that it showed. Hadn't she spent all of Sunday studying, working like a lunatic to take her mind off other, more pressing things? But now she came to think of it, she did feel different this morning. A bit more alert. The world was a better place.

She decided to confide. 'I went out with Ross on Saturday night. Well, I didn't intend to, but he found out I was going to a concert and he got the next place to me.' She reached over for a biscuit as Merry coughed nervously. 'Afterwards he took me to a restaurant on the river and...' Merry coughed again, more loudly. Lyn looked up, saw her strained face, then turned and found Melissa standing in the doorway.

'I wouldn't want to interrupt your coffee break,' Melissa said coldly, 'but have you seen those observations from the lab?'

'Not up yet,' Lyn said promptly. 'I know they were expected but—'

'Perhaps you'd like to phone down and ask about them. They're needed urgently. And by the way, there's no need to spend quite so much time with that Fatima child. You're a doctor; we have nurses to do that kind of thing.'

'Of course, Melissa,' said Lyn, vowing to herself to pay no attention whatsoever.

So far it had all been professional and quite proper. But then Melissa said, 'Interesting that you should spend the evening with Ross. The last time I heard you speak on the subject I thought you said he was just the kind of man you didn't care for. You really should try to make up your mind.'

Lyn didn't know whether to defend herself or point out that it was none of Melissa's business. She didn't have to. Melissa swept out, and the door slammed behind her.

'Oh, dear,' said Lyn. 'I hope this is not going to cause problems on the ward, Merry. You don't need a couple of feuding women interfering with your work.'

Merry shook her head. 'There'll be no problems. Melissa may have faults, but she'd never be anything less than professional. Anyway, keep out of her way today and you won't see her for the rest of the week. She's taking some time off. You'll see a bit more of Ross—he's taking over her work.'

'Oh, good,' said Lyn dubiously. She wasn't sure how she would cope with Ross being so close.

In fact she coped with him as she had coped with all

her problems—by working extra hard. It was easy, when there was so much to learn.

'If you have an acute subdural haematoma, I don't know how you judge whether to cut a burr hole or go for a full craniotomy,' she told Ross. 'I didn't have a chance to ask Melissa.'

'An SHO doesn't need to know,' he told her.

'But I'm not going to stay an SHO for ever, you can bet on that. If you haven't time to tell me yourself, then tell me where to look it up.'

'I guess I've got time.' He sighed. 'I can always do without sleep for another night.'

At about eleven on Friday morning he found her sitting on Fatima's bed, trying to teach the little girl a few more English words from a picture book she had bought.

'Doctor's orders,' he told her. 'This is Friday, the day for taking things easy. You will have an elongated lunch-time and come to the pub with me.'

'But I can't do that! I've got to—'

He held up a silencing hand. 'What you've got to do is what you're told. May I say that the purpose of our visit to the pub is professional, not social and certainly not sexual. Well, not very sexual. There are things we have to discuss.'

'About work?' she queried.

'Very much about work. It may have escaped your notice, but I do take my professional teaching duties seriously.'

In fact she had noticed. House officers, medical students, nurses, anyone who might have an interest, Ross would include them in what he was doing, and make sure they understood how and why he was doing it.

To make sure she did as she was told, he picked her up at one o'clock and escorted her to the Mayflower. It wasn't as warm as it had been before, and there was a fair number of office workers having an end-of-week drink, but they found a quiet corner. He ordered ham sandwiches for them both, and lemonade and lime.

'So, how are you getting on?' he asked her. 'Still determined to specialise in neurology? It's not too late to change your mind, you know.'

'I love the work, and I'm more determined than ever to be a neurologist. I've sent off for details of the MRCS exam, and I'm going to have a stab at it as soon as I can.'

'Wait a minute, there's no hurry! You shouldn't be thinking of exams yet. Finish this year, then start thinking about the future.'

'I told you, I love the work. And I like to have a goal, something to focus on. Work makes my life easier.'

She hadn't meant to say that. She saw his eyes flicker towards her, realised that she had given him an opening.

'I've watched you this week,' he said flatly. 'It's not something that I've ever said to anyone before, but you work too hard. You work as if you're driven. No one can carry on as you do, and, if you do, in time you'll have a breakdown.'

'No, I won't,' she said feebly. Then she picked up her ham roll and took a great bite. He couldn't expect her to talk while she was eating.

He looked at her approvingly. 'I like a girl who eats well,' he said. 'But don't think that you can avoid my questions that way.'

'I don't eat too much!' she tried to protest without scattering crumbs all over the table.

'I didn't say you did. Now, I've got a confession to make. You told me that Merry was on your ward last year when...'

'When Gavin was killed,' she finished for him.

'Yes. Well, it was most unprofessional, but I tried to get her to talk about you. How you took things, what effect it had on you. I told her that I was concerned about you.'

'I'll bet you didn't get very far.'

He shook his head ruefully. 'You're right, I didn't. Merry is a loyal friend. But she did agree with me. She thinks you work too hard.' He leaned across the table so she couldn't avoid looking at him. 'She said you nearly killed yourself with overwork. You worked as if you were trying to do more than just forget what had happened. Why did you work so hard, Lyn?'

'It wasn't just his being killed, I...' She checked herself; she had to tell this story just right. 'I've always been able to lose myself in work, ever since I was a small girl. Perhaps that's how I managed to pass my exams, because I didn't get too much schooling. I remember lying in a tent when I was thirteen, wrapped up in my sleeping bag and reading a textbook by the aid of a torch. Rain was beating on the tent.'

'There's nothing more evocative than the sound of rain on a tent,' he told her.

'Not while you're studying.'

He studied her a minute, and then said, 'You were going to tell me more about what happened when Gavin died, and then you changed your mind. D'you want to tell me now?'

He was too quick!

'You can read me like a book,' she said, confused. 'I don't think I like it. You know what I'm feeling even when I'm not sure myself. It worries me.'

He reached over a reassuring hand and gripped her forearm. 'All I want to do is know you better. They say confession is good for the soul. You'll feel better if you share your troubles.'

'All right, perhaps I will...but not here and now... Ross, I think I want to go back to work now.' Now she had agreed that she was hiding something, she felt panic rising in her. Some things were best kept to herself!

'No problem, we'll both go back.'

He smiled, reassuring her. 'I'm not going to pressure you, Lyn.' His smile turned into something different, a mischievous grin. 'But you're now in my department and I'm responsible for your professional behaviour and conduct. It's my expert opinion that you need rest of a special kind. I'm prescribing a tonic, a short period of recuperation. You've no plans for Sunday?'

'Well, I was going to...'

'Don't you dare say you were going to catch up on your washing and clean the flat! Women's excuses!'

'All right,' she agreed. 'The flat and the washing can remain dirty.'

'Good. I'll pick you up Sunday morning, quite early, say about six o'clock. If you want you can sleep in the car.'

She was intrigued. 'Where are we going?'

'It's going to be a surprise. Wear something warm and not too expensive, and trainers. It'll be a complete change.'

'Not going up a mountain?'

'No. But it will be in the great outdoors. Looking forward to it?'

'Since I don't know what I'll be doing, I can't look forward to it,' she pointed out. 'But I suspect I shall enjoy myself.'

'I'm sure you will. I'll do the sandwiches and coffee bit, you can be a complete passenger.'

'You said that on purpose, didn't you?' she asked. 'You know the number of times women are relegated to sandwich-making duties.'

'I'm a New Man,' he said smugly. 'Well, parts of me are New Mannish.'

She decided she was looking forward to the day.

Lyn had never had any problem in getting up early. She rose, bathed and breakfasted and still was in plenty of time. It was while she was dressing that the first doubts crossed her mind. She found herself putting on the flannel shirt, the cord trousers, the thick sweater that she had used to wear when she'd been out to the mountains with Gavin. She hadn't worn any of them for nearly nine months. Bleak memories crowded her mind, and for a moment she wished she'd never agreed to go on this trip. Was she getting involved with another Gavin? She'd sworn she would never do that.

However, she had warned him, and had made her position clear. A house in the suburbs, two-point-four children, a husband who came home every night. She would settle for nothing else.

Then why are you going out with him today? a teasing voice asked. She was glad when she heard the noise of a diesel engine drawing up outside. It meant she didn't have to think of an answer for the question.

He had wanted an early start, so she wouldn't invite him in for coffee. She skipped downstairs and looked at the waiting vehicle dubiously. She had seen its kind so often before.

It was a long wheelbase Land Rover, battered and, by its number plate, not as old as it looked. Certainly it had not been used to drive quietly along the M25. It was the kind of vehicle used for expeditions through rough country. She'd been in this kind of vehicle, on those kind of expeditions, so often before.

He came round the front of the vehicle to greet her. She felt an odd chill of recognition. So far she had only seen him in his more or less formal hospital clothes, or in a dinner jacket. Now, like her, he was wearing cords, thick shirt and sweater, and she recognised how comfortable he seemed in them. This was the kind of man he was. Not the kind of man she wanted any more.

'I might have known you wouldn't have a highly polished Jaguar,' she told him.

He looked mournful. 'Afraid not. I am not highly polished, nor a Jaguar kind of man. Have I invited you out under false pretences, Lyn?'

'Just for once I'll forgive you.' She took his hand as she climbed into the Land Rover. Then she looked behind her. There were seats for a possible four more passengers, but they were designed to convert into twin bunks, and there were lockers, and a tiny stove and sink. Everything was so familiar.

He climbed in beside her, looked at her face and knew instantly what she was thinking. 'Bring back memories?' he asked. 'Other Land Rovers, other trips?'

'Yes,' she answered curtly. 'I haven't been in a vehicle like this for—quite some time.'

'Perhaps demons should be outfaced, Lyn,' he told her neutrally, and started the engine.

'Not all the memories are bad. I've had many happy times as…as well as the bad ones.'

'Good. Let's hope today will be happy. A new beginning, perhaps?'

'It's possible,' she said.

Because it was early, and Sunday, there wasn't too much traffic around and he negotiated his way expertly through the north London suburbs and eventually onto the A127 and so east. She was intrigued. In spite of what he had said, she had half expected a mad dash for the nearest mountains. But there were no mountains this way. 'Where are we going?' she asked.

'Travelling hopefully is better than arriving,' he told her. 'Wait and be surprised. In fact, this bit of countryside isn't too interesting. Why don't you have a sleep?'

She had slept so often in bumpy noisy vehicles like this. 'All right, I will,' she said, and reclined her seat.

She didn't sleep properly. But it was fun to doze there, and behind his seat there was stuffed an old oiled canvas jacket, smelling of rock and heather. That too brought back memories.

Finally the Land Rover stopped. She opened her eyes, and frowned. There was the smell of salt in the air, and the screech of gulls. 'We're at the seaside,' she mumbled, before pulling herself upright.

'We are indeed. I trust you brought your bucket and spade.'

She sat up. They were parked on a harbour wall, and in front of them were what seemed like a thousand yachts moored along a river. The sun was sparkling on the water and the breeze made ropes rattle against the masts. 'This is lovely,' she said. 'I've never been here before. Are we going for a walk round?'

He looked surprised. 'Certainly not. We're going for a sail. You can swim, can't you?'

'I can swim. Ross, this is so exciting.'

'We set off early so we could catch the tide. Come on, let's get aboard.'

He took two great canvas bags from the back of the Land Rover and led the way to a set of tall lockers. He unlocked one, took out a pair of oars and handed them to her. 'You can carry these.' Then she was given a couple of life jackets. A couple of minutes later she was wearing one of them, sitting warily opposite him in the stern of what seemed to be the tiniest of dinghies as he rowed out towards the series of moored yachts. The canvas bags were between them.

They bumped gently against the side of a dark blue painted yacht, called the *Mary Ann*. He tied the dinghy to it and then showed her how to vault aboard without falling into the water. There wasn't much she could do. She sat in the cockpit as he scrambled up and down, pulling sails out of bags, fastening them to the mast, tightening some ropes and loosening others. It all looked incredibly complicated. But in time they were ready. The flapping sails were hoisted, and pulled taut. Ross cast off the mooring, leaving the dinghy tied to it, and the yacht heeled over in the breeze.

'I forgot to ask you,' Ross said, 'do you get seasick? If you do we can motor inland for a while.'

She shook her head. 'I've never been sailing before, but I doubt it. I've never been travel-sick, and I've been on some quite rough cross-channel trips. And I don't want to go inland, I want to go out to sea.'

'Good. We'll just clear the estuary and then I'll show you how to steer.'

'Whose boat is it? Is it yours?'

''Fraid not, it belongs to my brother. But I borrow his boat and he borrows my Land Rover.'

'You've never talked about your family, have you? In fact, when I think of the conversations we've had, they've mostly been about me. I want to talk about you for a change.'

'We'll talk about me later. Right now I want you to

stop thinking and just feel. Sailing is the best antidote I
know to deep and gloomy thoughts. Just enjoy it.'

It *was* exhilarating. They seemed to be charging along
at a tremendous rate, even though she knew that it
couldn't be too fast. The *Mary Ann* felt alive, like a horse.
The sails hummed, the ropes tautened and slackened, they
bounced from wave to wave. When they were well out to
sea he taught her how to steer, how to respond to the
variations in wind, putting the tiller 'up' to catch it.

She was enjoying herself. She could feel the strains and
doubts of her weeks on the ward leaving her. She didn't
need to think any more about either work or her complicated private life. All she had to do was respond to the
beauty of the scenery and the excitement of sailing.

'We're going to gybe now,' Ross called. 'That means
this big spar, which is called a boom, is going to swing
across. Mind your head!'

She did as she was told. The boom swung across with
a jerk. For a moment the yacht hung motionless, then she
heeled over again and drove forward. 'That's called tack-
ing,' Ross told her.

The afternoon passed all too quickly. Ross had brought
two flasks, and she thought she had never tasted such fine
coffee. Lyn felt she was just getting the hang of how to
steer when Ross said they had to be heading back, they
had to catch the tide again. He guided them up the river,
and as the wind had largely died by this time they ghosted
up quietly, making twin ripples in the now mirror-like
water. Following his directions, she leaned overboard and
grabbed for the little orange buoy that marked their moor-
ings. When the yacht was moored there was the process
of taking down the sails again. This time she helped,
wanting to know what to do next time.

'Do we have to go straight ashore?' she asked him.

'Not at all. But you must be hungry. There are a number of good pubs and restaurants nearby, but if you want I've brought the makings of a meal and I can cook for you here.'

'I'm not hungry, I'm ravenous. And I want to eat here if we possibly can. It's so peaceful and beautiful.'

'You don't think it's the equivalent of squatting by a smoky fire grilling lumps of meat?' he teased.

She remembered that she had said that to him while they'd been overlooking the Thames, and felt slightly embarrassed. 'Perhaps it is. But I'll put up with it for once. Though how I'd feel if I had to spend a week on board, I don't know.'

'You get used to it. The galley below is quite efficient, so sit here and I'll go and see what I can cook.'

She felt that she ought to protest. 'Can't I do something, Ross? You've done everything so far. I'm not completely useless, you know.'

'No one would accuse you of being useless. But today is different, this is part of the treatment prescribed by your doctor—in this case, me. You are to take things entirely easy. In any case, you know what they say about two women in one kitchen—well, the galley isn't small, it's midget. Only room for one. Sit here and enjoy yourself.'

'All right, I will.' She had seen the galley, and, as he'd said, there was only room for one. The rest of the boat below was a miracle of compression. There were four bunks, an abundance of lockers and an assortment of nautical equipment. It looked neat and cosy at the moment, but what it would be like with four people living in it at sea, she didn't like to think.

It was so peaceful sitting out here in the cockpit. The sun was burning gold across the water, there was the ever-present cry of gulls and there was that seaside presence of salt and mud that she had only ever smelled in England.

'Start with an orange juice.' His head and shoulders appeared from the hatch down into the yacht, and he handed her a glass. 'Enjoying the view?'

She was. 'Very much so. You know, Ross, now that I'm relaxing I've realised just how uptight I've been getting. This has been so good for me.'

'Good. Look, it's not too cold, I thought we'd eat here in the open air. If you reach behind you there's a table-top stored there that fits across the cockpit.' She was fitting it as he ducked back to fetch the meal.

It was simple but satisfying. He'd fried chopped ham, eggs, and an assortment of vegetables. Then he'd slid the mixture into a couple of large buttered rolls and put the rolls in the oven for five minutes. To drink, there was more fruit juice. 'We're driving,' he apologised. 'So no alcohol.' It was a rule she very much approved of.

Afterwards there was coffee and a couple of cakes from an obviously expensive shop. 'Now,' she said, 'absolutely no argument. I am going to wash up. It's your turn to sit and admire the view.'

'But—'

'No buts. And don't say I won't know how—I've washed up in far worse places than this.'

'All right, then. But there's more coffee in the pot. I'll wait and we'll have the last drink together.'

'Suits me.' Washing up turned out to be no task at all, for Ross had largely cleaned as he'd cooked. She was back on deck inside five minutes, pouring coffee from the freshly warmed pot.

Dusk was drawing in, and lights were appearing in the cottages on the shoreline, and on one or two of the yachts. As yet there was no chill in the air. Both drank their coffee, sitting together in companionable silence. When he finished his coffee and stretched his arm behind her, it seemed the most natural thing in the world to lean against him, to put her head on his shoulder, to wrap her free arm round his waist.

'Why do I work so hard when I'm equally happy doing nothing?' she asked drowsily.

'Typical addict's complaint. Drinkers, smokers, drug addicts, all wonder why they bothered when they're cured. It's just that you're addicted to work.'

She smacked him, gently. 'If I'm addicted to work, then you're addicted to telling me about it. I get a sermon every time we meet.'

'It's because I care about my junior staff.' He put his other arm round her, and drew her to him. 'Are you comfortable there?'

'Wonderfully,' she told him.

They sat in silence a while longer, and then he said gently, 'Lyn, remember in the pub on Friday, you said there was something about what you felt when Gavin died. It was obviously troubling you. You wouldn't tell me then, do you want to tell me now?'

No, she didn't *want* to tell him. But she thought she was going to. Perhaps he was right, perhaps she had bottled up too much. 'I've never told this to anyone,' she said. 'I'm not even sure what it means.'

He didn't answer, just squeezed her. She went on, 'You know, there are all sorts of reactions to a...to a sudden death. There's disbelief, horror, sometimes even anger at the person who's died. They all take time to work through.'

'I know,' he said.

'Well, when I heard that Gavin was dead, I was shocked—devastated, in fact. He'd been the centre of my life. I'd had nothing to do with any other man than him for the past four years. And now he was gone. What was I to do? It was only about a week later that I started to feel something else.' She wasn't calm, at peace any more. She could feel the tears running down her face, her heart was beating faster, her breath coming quicker and quicker.

'Then I had to go to a memorial service to him. There was no proper funeral—he'd been buried in Borneo. And all his old friends whom I'd known so long, they all were there. They thought I was crying for him, but I wasn't. I'd just realised the emotion I was feeling, and it horrified me. It horrifies me still.'

'Tell me, Lyn,' he urged. 'You know you need to.'

'All right, I will! The emotion I felt was relief! During the four years that I knew him, whenever he had the chance he was away on some dangerous madcap expedition. Three of his friends died while I knew him, and all he did was laugh. Then he died, and I think I was half expecting it, and at long last I didn't have to worry any more. I felt relief, Ross! I would never have to be sick with worry again!'

She leaned against him, sobbing. 'Never again,' he heard her muffled voice. 'Never, never, never worry again.'

They sat without speaking then, the only sound the gurgle of the ebbing tide as it eddied round the hull. Her head slowly drooped, and he eased her so that she rested on his lap. His canvas coat was on the side of the cockpit, and gently he drew it round her to protect her from the evening air. Against his thigh he could feel the rise and fall of her chest; it slowed further and he knew she was asleep. As a doctor he knew it was a common reaction to stress, to pain, physical and mental. The body was a machine that could only take so much. When it was overtaxed it would shut down.

After perhaps an hour he felt her stir. She pushed herself upright, rubbed at her eyes and yawned. 'I fell asleep,' she said, sounding bewildered. 'I didn't know I was that tired.'

'It's the sea air,' he said, knowing that it wasn't. 'It makes everybody sleepy.'

'Perhaps.' She was coming awake now. 'Ross, I told you things I've never told anyone before. I feel... vulnerable. And I shouldn't have troubled you with my problems.'

'Do you feel better for telling me?' he asked.

She considered. 'Yes,' she said. 'D'you know, I think I do?'

'Good. Now, it's time we were getting back. See, it's dark.'

She looked round a moment. 'This has been a wonderful day, Ross. Will you bring me back again some time?'

'I'd really like to,' he said.

CHAPTER FIVE

THERE was more traffic on the road going home. Apparently much of London had decided to take advantage of the fine weather and travel to the seaside. After they had driven for an hour, Lyn said, 'That's the third time you've yawned—you're getting tired. Pull over, and I'll drive for a while. It's your turn to sleep.'

Ross looked at her uncertainly. 'You'll drive? This is quite a big vehicle, you might find—'

'Stop thinking that the only car a woman can drive is a Mini. You've got power steering, and, besides, I've probably spent more hours driving a Land Rover than you have. Now, if you carry on you'll be a danger on the road.'

'Yes, miss,' he muttered, but he pulled over anyway and offered her the driver's seat. It took her a while to adjust the seat height and mirrors, but then she moved confidently onto the road, and soon was moving as quickly as the traffic would allow.

For perhaps five minutes, he watched her. Then he said, 'I was a fool to doubt you. Everything I've seen you do, you do well. Can you find your way back to your flat?'

'Easily. Don't forget, I live in north London.'

'Wake me if there's a problem.' As she had done, he reclined his seat, and soon was apparently asleep. She felt pleased with his confidence in her.

It was nearly eleven when they drew up outside her flat. He woke at once as they stopped. The last time he had brought her home she had not wanted him to come in with her, but this time she rather wished he would. 'It's getting late but you can come in for a coffee if you like,' she said. 'It'll wake you up for the journey down to Lizzie's.'

'I'd like a coffee,' he said. 'More than that, I want to see where you live.'

She was curious. 'Why?'

'The...surroundings people choose for themselves say something about their characters. I'll know you better when I've seen inside your flat.'

'I think you know me pretty well already,' she told him.

He was more interested in the flat than he was in coffee, so she started the percolator and showed him round. First, however, there was one fact to be made quite clear. 'I lived here with Gavin. We were going to get married and we didn't see any reason to have two homes while we were waiting.'

'Seems eminently sensible,' he assured her. 'But you didn't want to move out when he died?'

She waved him over to the living-room window, showing him the view of the lights of London below. If anything, it was more impressive at night than in the day. 'I picked this flat because I fell in love with this view. I was determined I wasn't going to be driven out by ghosts, by memories. And I asked myself, what would I have wanted, if I had died leaving the flat to Gavin? I would have wanted him to stay here. In fact, there was a dual life insurance on the place, so it was paid off in full. The flat is mine now.'

'I like it.' He looked round the décor. 'But this isn't a man's choice of furnishing. You decorated, made a lot of changes, didn't you?'

'I made it mine,' she told him.

He looked at the bathroom, the kitchen, her bedroom,

the living room. He admired them all. 'There's quite a big roof space as well,' she told him. 'There's a ladder that pulls down. It's handy for storing stuff that you don't need very often.' And then they were left with the one room she hadn't showed him. He didn't ask, merely looked at her expressionlessly.

She told him what she had told Merry. 'This room is locked. In it I put all the things that had belonged to Gavin, all the reminders of our life together. I was starting a new life.'

'Why lock it?' he asked. 'Is that where you have placed the ghosts? How long since you looked inside?'

He was being tough with her. She would be tough back. 'I've not looked inside for a couple of months,' she told him, 'but I'll fetch the key now.'

He watched in silence as she fetched the key from the drawer in the kitchen, unlocked the door and threw it open. Together they looked at the dusty furniture, the boxes of papers and pictures. Saddest of all was a pair of old climbing boots.

'I'll get rid of most of it soon,' she said, knowing that her voice was shaking slightly. 'I just haven't had time to sort through it all, really.'

Gently he pulled her away, took the key from her hand and relocked the door. 'I'm sorry,' he said. 'I'm pushing you through a lot of feelings that you're not quite ready for. You need more time.'

'No. Sometimes people need a push. I'm glad you made me open the door. It's only old furniture and things for which there now is little use.' She took the key from him, and unlocked the door. 'From now on that door stays unlocked. The room is part of my flat.'

It was time to move onto something else. She took him into the tiny kitchen alcove, and poured him a coffee. 'Just a small one,' he said. 'I should go soon. You're at work tomorrow, and I'm back at Everton Heights.'

'I'll be working with Melissa,' Lyn said, thinking that it wouldn't be as much fun as working with Ross.

'So you will.' He drained his cup, stood, moved towards the door, and she followed him.

In the hall he turned, and took her by the shoulders. 'Lyn, I think I'm getting too old to be seen kissing people in doorways. So…' He pulled her gently towards him.

His last kiss had been sweet, like the kiss of a relative. This kiss started sweetly, too. But soon there was passion as she clutched him closer to her. It broke over her like a dam bursting. This was what she needed, had been missing. She needed a man like Ross, to hold her, to kiss her like this, to—

He broke away from her, and she knew he felt the same way as she did. He said, 'This isn't the time and place. But we'll be seeing each other again, Lyn.'

'I've enjoyed today so much,' she told him. 'You've given me so much to think about.'

'Take things easy, sweetheart. A little progress at a time.' He kissed her again, quickly. 'I'll ring you tomorrow.'

When he had gone she undressed, ran herself a bath and slid into it. She had enjoyed today, and there was so much to think about. The first thing, of course, was Ross. She had never met a man who affected her so much. And yet she'd sworn to herself never to have anything to do with a man like him. It was a problem. For now she would shelve it.

'Hello, Doctor Lyn,' said Fatima, smiling.

'Hello, Fatima,' Lyn said, and then tried a mouthful of strange sounds she had been taught by the Arab staff

nurse. It was supposed to be a traditional greeting, and
Lyn thought she'd mastered it. Not so Fatima. She tried
hard not to giggle but couldn't quite manage it.

'It is…' she said, and produced what Lyn thought were
exactly the same sounds.

Lyn tried again—and this time Fatima indicated that
things were a bit better. If she has as much trouble learning English as I have learning Arabic, then she has my
sympathy, Lyn thought. It's harder than French.

'Just a few comics,' she said to Fatima. 'If you don't
read them you can look at the pictures.'

Fatima reached for the comics happily. Sometimes Lyn
wondered what impression she had of English society
from them, but they kept her contented.

'I'll drop in and see you later,' she said, and the now-
engrossed Fatima waved at her. She was making good
progress, there appeared to be no complications and there
was apparently no permanent damage because of the compression of the brain. Fatima had been lucky.

'Had a good weekend?' Melissa asked as they checked
through the series of reports that had come back from the
lab.

Lyn paused before answering. She would have preferred Melissa not to know what she had been doing, but
she wasn't going to lie. 'As a matter of fact, I went out
sailing with Ross on Sunday,' she said. 'He'd borrowed
his brother's boat.'

Just for a moment Melissa stopped leafing through the
reports, but her voice was calm and quite pleasant as she
went on, 'I thought you didn't care for that sort of thing?'

'I've done a lot of it in my time,' Lyn said cautiously.
'I just don't care for men who wander off to foreign parts
leaving their women behind.'

Melissa wasn't insensitive. 'That was said with feeling,'

she said, 'as if you meant it, you'd felt it. Was there a man like that in your past?'

'Yes,' said Lyn. 'But I'm not going to talk about it.'

He was only in for the afternoon. 'If you have time,' Ross said, 'you could assist me in an operation. Right temporal lobectomy. Barbara, aged thirteen—she's been referred to me by a hospital in the Midlands. I've had her in Everton Heights but I want to operate here.'

'I'd love to assist,' Lyn said, delighted, 'but tell me something about the case.'

'She suffers from psychomotor epilepsy. There's a small tumour in the lobe, and I think removing it will cure the epilepsy. I've done an MRI scan, an EEG and assessed speech and memory. You can look at the notes if you like.'

'I *would* like,' Lyn said. 'I thought surgery for epilepsy was a bit unusual.'

'It is. But I'm convinced there's a good chance of Barbara being cured. And curing an epileptic is wonderful news—for the family as well as the patient. Half-past two, then?'

Watching Ross operate was an education. Everything he did appeared so simple and so easy. The craniotomy came first, and he let her drill the initial burr holes. Then he eased the flap of bone backwards and the brain was revealed. His movements were so deft as he cut, retracted, separated. Then, marvellously quickly, it was done. 'Easy, isn't it?' he asked her.

'No,' she said, 'I don't think it is.'

'I've got a confession,' Ross said when he phoned her at home two nights later.

She was glad that he had phoned. She got a buzz at the

sound of his voice. But—a confession? 'What sort of confession?'

'You know the hospital is having a big party for Halloween? The staff association has been working at it for weeks.'

'I think I've heard about it.' What was he going to say? Her heart beat a little faster.

'Well, I've been invited. Melissa came over specially to see me, she said her father and brother were coming to the do, and would I like to join them at their table? She says her father would very much like to chat to me and I feel a bit honoured, because he's quite an eminent cardiologist. So I said yes, I'd love to meet him.'

'I'm sure you'll have a wonderful time,' Lyn said desolately.

'Wait a minute, woman. Don't jump to conclusions. This is the confession bit. I told her that I was flattered, but that I'd already asked you to accompany me. Which I would have got round to. Anyway, Melissa said that was no problem at all, wouldn't you like to come and join them too? She said there was no chance of Henry turning up, otherwise it would be nice to see the department all together. How d'you feel?'

Lyn had mixed feelings. First, she was glad that Ross wanted to go with her. There was still her long-term worry, of course, that he was not her kind of man. But she wanted to go to the party with him and she would have preferred to go with him alone. She wasn't sure about joining Melissa's party—but the woman hadn't been half as unpleasant to her as she could have been. And Ross seemed quite to want to meet the father.

'I'd love to go in a gang,' she said. 'It's always more fun if there are lots of people together.'

'Good, I'll phone Melissa. Are you missing me, Lyn?'

'Yes,' she said, 'but I'm coping with it very well.' She heard him laughing as he rang off.

Next day she found a quiet moment and told Merry about the party invitation. Surprisingly, Merry was more suspicious than she had been herself. 'Melissa's accustomed to getting her own way, Lyn,' she said. 'She doesn't like being crossed. I told you she'd never do anything unprofessional, and I know she's a good doctor, if a bit cool, but she needs to be watched.'

'Surely you're exaggerating?' Lyn said.

'If she thinks she's right, then she can be quite vicious.' Merry looked troubled. 'I shouldn't tell you this, but I will. There was trouble with a nurse on the ward here before I came. I gather she wasn't much of a nurse, idle and careless, but she might have made something of herself. Possibly. Anyway, one day she didn't follow Melissa's instructions properly. She didn't give a dose of drugs when they were needed, and a baby became quite ill. Very properly Melissa didn't say anything until there had been an official enquiry, and the nurse found at fault. Then she found that my predecessor, the sister before I came, was going to give the nurse another chance. Not a second one, but about a tenth chance. So Melissa told the sister and the nurse that the nurse might as well leave at once. No matter what tribunals, appeals, systems were in place, she was going to see that the girl was finished as a nurse. She resigned the same day.'

Lyn thought about this story. The more she thought, the more she found it entirely believable. 'So what d'you think of the story?' she asked Merry.

'Well, I wouldn't have the nerve to try such a thing. But from what I can gather, the ward was a happier, better place when the nurse had gone. Just pointing out that Melissa can be ruthless.'

'Hmm,' muttered Lyn.

She hadn't really calmed down when later that afternoon Melissa approached her on her ward, smiled at Fatima and said, 'I do hope you'll join us at the Halloween party. Ross said he was coming with you and it would be nice if we could be together. My father and brother are coming, too.'

'I'm really looking forward to it,' said Lyn, now feeling thoroughly ashamed.

On Friday night she went to tea with Merry and her husband. Richard had finished his medical course and was in his third year training to be a GP. Lyn had met him before.

'He's not called a trainee any more,' Merry said with a giggle. 'Apparently some young doctor somewhere thought it a bit degrading after all those years' work. So now he's called a registrar.'

'Seems fair enough,' Lyn said. 'What's he going to do when he qualifies?'

'He's been offered a junior partnership in the practice he's working at. He's very happy there, so he's going to accept.'

She led Lyn through to the back of the house, seated her in the large, open-plan kitchen and draped a cloth over her shoulder and front. 'Now, you're going to have to work for your supper while I finish off the casserole.'

From a cot she took the gently grumbling baby, placed him in Lyn's arms and handed her a bottle. 'You can feed the young master and I'll see what I can do to feed us.'

Lyn watched happily as the baby's eyes twitched open and shut, as the little pink mouth rooted for the teat and then grabbed it with such enthusiasm. 'You know, we see too many ill babies,' she said to Merry. 'We tend to forget they are in the minority. I think every baby doctor should be frequently exposed to a set of healthy children. It gets the perspectives right.'

From the front of the house came the sound of someone entering, and seconds later Richard entered the kitchen. He kissed his wife, put a hand on Lyn's shoulder to stop her getting up, bent and kissed Nathan's head, then kissed Lyn on the cheek. 'All this kissing,' he said. 'What a lovely way to spread germs.'

Lyn laughed. She didn't know Richard very well but she liked him. He was a short, stubby man with twinkling eyes and an ability to get on with people. Before training as a doctor he had been a nurse, and Lyn had always thought that the double skills were very useful.

Richard poured himself a sherry, lifted the decanter and looked at Merry and Lyn. Both shook their heads. 'How's being a GP?' Lyn asked. 'Merry says you're enjoying it.'

'I am. Totally different from hospital work. It teaches you that...' he thought for a moment '...that little things are very important. If you're in hospital, then that's the central fact of your life. You think most about getting better. But if you're being treated out of hospital, having to get on with your life, your work, and your family, then your illness or whatever has to take second place.'

This interested Lyn, for she'd never thought of it like that before. 'Go on,' she said curiously.

'Well, you know the number of people who start on antibiotics, and then think they're getting better and just don't bother to finish the course?'

Lyn did know. It was a constant concern among medical staff, because not finishing a course of antibiotics could lead to a resistance to the drug if it needed to be used later. 'It makes me angry,' she said. 'We always warn people about it.'

'I used to feel angry, too. But now I have just a touch

of sympathy. Simply remembering to take a tablet three times a day can be too much for some busy people.'

'But surely their health is important!'

'Of course it is. But so is the rest of their life. That's why I said that little things are important. When a GP gets a new patient and takes a history, it shouldn't just be of an illness, it should be of an entire lifestyle. There might be an ideal treatment for a condition. But the patient's lifestyle might make that treatment impossible.'

Lyn thought about this. She could see Richard's nursing training coming through, and thought it was a good thing. 'But does a GP have time to take a history of a lifestyle?' she asked.

Richard laughed. 'Now that is the important question. I'm afraid the answer is often no.'

Lyn had finished feeding the baby now, burped him with some success and taken a tissue and wiped his mouth.

'Shall I take him now?' Richard asked, and sat with his son on his shoulder, rocking him gently. Lyn thought they looked so contented.

There was silence for a while. Richard had a quick peep inside the baby's nappy, and decided that no change was needed. He rocked a little longer, and then laid the baby carefully in his cot. 'Perhaps he'll leave us in peace to have our meal,' he said cheerfully. 'Perhaps.'

Merry was now busy in the kitchen annex, laying the table. They would eat in a few minutes. Lyn thought of her past few weeks, of meeting Ross, of being forced to think about things that she had pushed to the back of her mind. It was time to lay ghosts. Richard could help her.

'You trained with Gavin Bell, my fiancé,' she stated baldly.

Richard looked at her warily. 'Yes, I did. I was very sorry to hear that he—'

Lyn waved impatiently. 'I'm getting over it now, Richard. Don't worry, I'm not going to get upset. But you and he were together, three years ahead of me. I want to know what he was like, how other people got on with him in the hospital.' She paused, thinking how to explain what she wanted. 'I was in love with him, I was going to marry him, but I'm now not sure what he was really like. Please, Richard, I need to know.'

She could tell that he wasn't comfortable with the question. He paused before replying, and Lyn said with a touch of humour, 'I know what you're doing. You're being a GP, trying to assess whether the patient should be allowed to know everything.'

'Don't think that complete knowledge is bound to free you, Lyn. I've had cases when patients demanded to know facts and then been destroyed by them.'

'I'll take my chance,' she said.

'Very well. I wouldn't have said Gavin was a friend, because socially we moved in different circles. He was a very clever doctor, far cleverer than me. He remembered everything, and had no problem studying. He was always on the move, whatever he did. We used to call him Quicksilver.'

'Quicksilver.' She'd never heard this before. But there again, there were areas of his life that she knew little about. It was a good nickname, so right for him. Bright, shining, never still. 'But?' she asked.

Richard looked confused. 'Why but?'

'Your tone suggested you had reservations about him. What were they?'

'No, no, I liked him. He was everybody's friend. He'd help anyone, nothing was too much trouble for him.'

She could tell there was more, but that Richard didn't want to upset her. 'Please,' she said. 'I've got to come to terms with his death. At times I feel almost—resentful of him dying. I feel I didn't know him.'

Merry had come in, sat by her husband, took his hand. 'Tell her, Richard,' she said. 'She deserves to know.'

Richard was still unhappy; Lyn could tell he was picking his words with care. 'Of all the doctors I trained with…he was the one most likely to get killed in the way he did. For some branches of medicine he was far too impetuous. He was a risk-taker. In some circumstances that's a good thing—he would have been a good battlefield surgeon, for instance. But not most medicine.' Richard screwed up his eyes. 'I think there was a streak of…selfishness in his character. That's an odd thing to say about a man who helped others so much.'

'I know exactly what you mean about selfishness,' Lyn said quietly. 'Joe, thank you so much for telling me. You don't know how you've helped.'

'Food,' said Merry. 'Richard, you can fetch us a bottle of wine.'

CHAPTER SIX

BECAUSE of her baby Merry decided she wouldn't go to the Halloween Ball, but one of the staff nurses told Lyn all about it. It was to take place in the physiotherapy department's gymnasium, with all the equipment temporarily moved out. Usually the staff association went to considerable trouble, and the event would be well run and popular.

Lyn forgot her misgivings about going with Melissa, and concentrated on deciding on a costume. She loved dressing up, perhaps because so much of her youth had been spent in drab, functional clothes. Each day she took pride and pleasure in dressing well, and now the idea of pretending to be someone else, someone exotic, thrilled her.

Ross phoned her. 'Are you going in fancy dress?' he asked her cautiously. 'Do we have to?'

'Yes, I am going in fancy dress, and, yes, you have to as well,' she told him firmly. 'You're not to be a party pooper.'

'But I've no idea what to go as,' he wailed.

'Get an idea,' she told him. 'One thing is certain: I'm not going to dance with anyone who isn't dressed up.'

'I'm supposed to be the SR, and you the humble SHO,' he grumbled. 'Why don't you think that everything I say is automatically right?'

'I do think that everything you say is automatically right. You invited me to a fancy dress ball so I'm coming in fancy dress.'

'I think I'll come as Bluebeard. He kept women locked in his castle, and disposed of them if they didn't do exactly as he wished. Would you like to come as one of his slave girls? A costume of nothing but bits of gauze and a pearl choker? That's an idea I like.'

'In your dreams,' she told him. 'I've made up my mind. I'll come as an Eskimo.'

'Then I'll wear my polar-bear suit. Look forward to seeing you anyhow.'

She liked it when he phoned. Most of the time they had a cheerful, joking exchange, with no reference to anything serious. Without saying anything, they had both decided that certain matters were best left for the moment.

'I'm really looking forward to dressing up,' she told Melissa the next day. 'Have you decided on a costume yet?'

The question seemed to take Melissa by surprise. 'Not really,' she said. 'Perhaps I'll—'

'I was talking to Ross on the phone last night,' Lyn interrupted. 'He said he hadn't quite decided on a costume yet, but he was obviously taking a lot of time to get it right.'

This was rather a perversion of what had actually been said. But it had the desired effect. Melissa stiffened. 'There's a costumier's I know,' she said. 'I'll give them a ring tonight.'

Good. Now, whatever Lyn chose to wear, she wouldn't have to sit with a Melissa dressed in the latest evening gown. But what would she wear?

'I want to look specially good,' she told Merry. 'All I've done recently is work. I want to show I can enjoy myself as well. Going to this ball is a sort of a symbol. And I don't want a dress that looks good but that I can't dance in. I want to leap about a bit.'

'Good idea.' Merry surveyed her critically. 'If you've got it, flaunt it. Sometimes I think you dress just a bit too conventionally. Make something of those legs and that bust. Let people see them.'

'Well, up to a point,' Lyn said.

In the end it was her mother who came up with a suggestion. Her parents had just arrived home from Scotland and she had phoned Lyn for a casual chat. Lyn had told her her problem.

'No problem, dear. When we were in Mexico a couple of years ago we went to a celebration of the Day of the Dead. You know the Mexicans make a lot of it. Well, a lot of the girls there were wearing what they called a ghost dress. They're made of some silky material, very thin, and covered with paintings of skeletons and so on. And there's a big arching headdress to go with it. I bought one, I don't know why; I'll certainly never wear it. I'll send it to you.'

Lyn smiled to herself. Her mother was constantly fancying clothes abroad, buying them and then realising that never would she dare wear them.

'Thanks, Ma,' she said, 'it sounds just right. Listen, I'm working for an SR who really wants to meet you both. Can we come down some time soon? He's another wanderer in foreign parts...'

The dress arrived two days later. Lyn took it from its box, shook it out and blinked a little. It was certainly an—exciting dress. She had wanted to wear something startling, attractive, and this was both of those. The material was a soft, clingy silk, the designs on it bold and pagan. But it was sleeveless and low cut, and the long skirt was slashed to the top of the right thigh. She took off the blouse and trousers she had been wearing and wriggled into the dress. It did more than fit her; it clung to her. She pulled on the headdress and stared at herself in the full-length mirror. No longer was she a conventionally dressed young lady doctor. She looked like some barbaric queen.

There were more decisions to be taken on the night of the ball. To be safe and proper she should wear a full slip under the dress. But she didn't want to. The dress just didn't hang right when she did. It was meant to cling to the body. She threw the slip aside, and compromised by searching her underwear drawer for sturdy bra and briefs, instead of the silky scraps she generally wore.

Ross was working till the last minute; he had phoned her and apologised but explained that there was no way he could pick her up. 'Got a glioma that must come out soonest,' he'd said, referring to a brain tumour, 'and I know it'll be a long job.'

'No problem,' she had said lightly. 'We'll meet in the doctors' lounge. Melissa's going to wait for us there.'

The medical staff might be going to let their hair down to a certain extent, but there were limits. Nurses and technicians had joyfully agreed to meet in their fancy costumes in pubs near the hospital, but the doctors had felt that appearing like that in public would compromise their dignity. They would meet in the slightly stuffy hospital doctors' lounge.

Lyn took a taxi to the hospital, wrapped in a long coat and with her headdress in a bag. Then she nipped into the ladies' cloakroom, made a few last-minute adjustments to her make-up and put on her headdress.

There were others in fancy dress around her, and after looking at them she felt slightly better. There was a size-fourteen-or-more sister somehow crammed into a size twelve fairy's dress. There was an eighteenth-century lady with the necessary high silver wig, and the equally necessary vast amount of bosom showing. Display seemed to be the order of the day. She walked along to the doctors' lounge.

Melissa saw her as soon as she entered, and vigorously waved her over. She was dressed as Morticia out of *The Addams Family*, in a long black dress with a long black wig. Her face was Pan-Cake white with heavily made-up eyes and a dark red lipstick. She looked striking. By her side two other people stood as Lyn approached.

Melissa was being friendly, putting everyone at their ease. 'This is Lyn,' she said, 'the SHO who does all of my hard work. Lyn, that's a wonderful dress! This is my father, Sir Sidney Yates.'

Sir Sidney was a tall, smiling bald man, dressed in surgeons' greens, with an abundance of rather suspect bloodstains. On his belt was hung a selection of silver saws.

'My daughter loves that ''Sir'',' he said, squeezing Lyn's hand. 'I think she wants to be Dame Melissa. I couldn't think of a fancy dress, Lyn, so I came in my working clothes.'

'And this is my brother Simon,' Melissa went on. 'I'm afraid he's a doctor, too.' There was something a little odd about Melissa's tone, but Lyn couldn't quite decide what it was.

She turned to shake hands with the third member of the little party. So far he had remained in the background, in the shadow of a pillar. Now he stepped forward, and Lyn gasped. Simon Yates was the most beautiful man she had ever seen!

He was dressed as Apollo, or some other Greek god. Guessing by the way it hung, Lyn thought the white toga he was wearing was not made out of a sheet. Its whiteness contrasted with the tanned arms and one naked shoulder. His curly blond hair held a little silver circlet. And his face!

'So pleased to meet you, Lyn,' he said, 'and may I say that your dress is truly stunning?'

'Thank you,' she mumbled. 'I like yours, too.'

He placed a hand on her arm, and guided her to a seat on a couch as if he were handling delicate porcelain. 'I'll get us all something to drink,' he said. 'Lyn, what would you like? And I gather a Dr McKinnon will be here soon—do you know what he might like?'

She thought it was a considerate question, and suggested they both have a glass of red wine, before she turned to talk to Sir Sidney.

'My old friend Henry keeping you busy?' he asked. 'That man works like a lunatic. You might not see so much of it in the hospital, but he's on countless committees and so on. I've told him that if he doesn't ease up he'll end up on my table.'

'He's always got time for my little problems,' she told him truthfully. 'He's a very good teacher.'

'Never learned how to say no to a request. That's vital if you're to have a happy doctor's life, Lyn. Ever thought of a career as a cardiac surgeon?'

She had, but had been discouraged by the competition. 'It's hard to get into,' she pointed out. 'Everybody wants to be a heart surgeon, and there still seems to be a prejudice against women.'

'I'm afraid there probably is. What it is, we're trying to keep quiet the fact that heart surgery is easy. Just plumbing. If there's a dripping tap in our house, who d'you think gets called to fix it? The real hard medical work is done by people like you and Melissa and Henry.'

She decided she liked Sir Sidney. Unlike a number of other consultants she had met, he was not consumed by admiration for his own success.

Simon returned with a tray of drinks, handed them out

and sat by her on the couch. 'I must ask, what are you?' he said. 'Or is it just something that you dreamed up?'

She explained about her parents, and the dress from Mexico. Sir Sidney had heard of Jack and Jo Webster, but Simon had not. 'It certainly is unusual,' Simon said, running his finger across one of the signs on her back. 'These patterns are patched on, aren't they?'

Sir Sidney leaned over and peered at her front. 'Needlework isn't as good as mine,' he said. 'This woman would be no good at aorta work.'

All Lyn's previous worries had by now disappeared. It was a cheerful, good-humoured group; she was going to enjoy herself. Even Melissa was making an effort to unbend. All that was needed was for Ross to arrive.

'Anyway, how are you getting on with my evil big sister?' Simon asked. 'I don't suppose you could put a Mexican curse on her, could you? You know she's blighted my career? I had to become a doctor just to compete with her. When I was younger, I wanted to be a jet pilot.'

Melissa leaned over to thump him, and Lyn joined in the general laughter. It was obvious that there was a lot of relaxed love between the two.

A voice said, 'Sorry I'm late,' and she looked up. Even though she knew who it was, her heart lurched. Every time she met him this happened. Ross was smiling down at them. He was dressed as an American gangster, in a tight pinstriped suit, a black silk shirt with a white tie and a fedora over one eye. 'I couldn't think of a fancy dress, so I came in my normal medical outfit,' he said. 'There was an article in today's paper—doctors are holding the country to ransom.'

He touched Lyn on the shoulder, and then walked round to sit next to Sir Sidney, where there was a spare seat. Sir Sidney shook his hand vigorously. 'That article you published last month about electrical impulses in the brain stem,' he said. 'Very interesting, a good basis for more research. Now, you know I'm particularly interested in arrhythmia, why hearts go into say, atrial fibrillation. It struck me that the impulses—'

'Dad!' said Melissa sternly. 'You're talking shop!'

'I enjoy talking shop. Besides, young Ross here is fascinated by what I'm saying. Aren't you, Ross?'

'As a matter of fact, I am.' The two men moved their chairs a little closer together, and soon were engrossed in their learned conversation.

Melissa looked at her watch. She winked at Lyn, and said, 'We've finished our drinks, let's go downstairs to find our table. We can stack this pair in a corner somewhere and let them carry on with their talk.'

'That seems a good idea,' said Simon. So they moved.

Someone had gone to a lot of trouble to make the gym suitably spooky for Halloween. There were black and orange streamers, Jack-o-lanterns on the tables, gravestones here and there. Most people had picked their costumes with care, Lyn saw a Mad Hatter, a Roman centurion, and more than a handful of ghouls.

The room was dimly lit, but as she entered it Lyn felt that she was moving out of darkness into light. For the past nine months her life had consisted of nothing but misery and work. Now she was going to enjoy herself. For nine months she had neither looked at a man, nor thought about one—except Ross, in the past few weeks, she reminded herself. But here she was now, in the company of two most attractive men, and enjoying the attention she was receiving. People were noticing her dress, too. She looked far different from the usually demure Dr Webster!

They found their table, and Ross set off at once to fetch another round of drinks. Lyn asked for something long, non-alcoholic and cold. She guessed that this was going to be a warm night, and she didn't want to spoil it by getting dehydrated.

'Let's dance,' said Simon, and led her onto the floor.

She'd half forgotten how much she enjoyed dancing, it had been so long. When she'd been with Gavin she hadn't danced much, because his idea of a good evening had been to sit talking in the pub with a bunch of his mates.

Simon held her close. He was dressed in a toga, she in a sleeveless dress, so there were naked bits of their bodies that rubbed together. His skin was warm. She supposed she liked it—it was nice—but she pushed him gently away, and he moved at once. 'I'm really enjoying this, dancing with you,' he said.

Surprisingly, though, for such an athletic-looking man, he wasn't a very good dancer. He tried—someone had taught him some steps—but he didn't move with the naturalness that Lyn needed. He had little sense of rhythm, but he smiled at her, and Lyn was happy.

The music came to an end, and something new was starting. Most people stayed on the floor and Simon wanted to. But, 'Let's go back to the table,' she said. 'I'm getting rather warm and I'd like a drink.' Of course, he took her at once.

'I really needed that,' she told Ross as she sipped the iced lemon drink he had brought her.

'Glad you like it, I'm having the same myself.' He lifted his glass to show her.

'Good. You'd better keep fit, because I haven't danced for years, and I love it. So you're in for a long hard night.'

'Then let's start right now.' He led her onto the floor. The band had changed tempo and were playing something slow and dreamy. She slid into his arms and they moved gently to the music. 'Missed me?' he asked.

'Certainly have. Life on the ward isn't the same without you. You're a better teacher than Melissa.'

'I asked if you'd missed *me*! Not your medical tutor.'

She pretended to think…then squeezed him. 'Yes, I suppose I have.' More seriously, she went on, 'I've been doing a lot of thinking. I talked to someone who used to know Gavin. I'm beginning to rethink things, get my life back.'

'I'm so pleased,' he said sincerely, and they danced in silence for a moment. 'And while I have the chance,' he went on, 'let me say what an enchanting dress that is.' He looked down. 'It's good to see so much of you.' She blushed.

'I felt quite peeved when I saw you dancing with the Greek god, bare skin to bare skin.'

'Ross McKinnon! In anyone less relaxed than you I'd say that was jealousy.'

He looked mock affronted. 'Me! Be jealous? Why, have I any cause to be?'

In a judicious voice, she said, 'He's certainly a gorgeous hunk.' They danced slowly behind a pillar, where she took his head in her hands, pulled it down and quickly kissed him. 'But after mature reflection I think I prefer you.'

They went back to their table. Melissa demanded to dance with Ross, and Simon led Lyn onto the floor again.

She had to admit to herself that he was more than just extraordinarily good-looking, he was a charming man as well. Once again he held her slightly too close, once again she eased him away. 'Sorry,' he said. 'By that I mean I'm sorry you're pushing me away. I was rather enjoying our various bare bits making contact.' She had to laugh.

He didn't just dance, he talked to her as well. He wanted to know about her private life, but she wouldn't tell him. Then he asked about her course, about where she'd trained, about her plans for the future, and she found herself telling him this. He was an easy, relaxed companion.

'I'll bet you're good at taking histories,' she told him. 'No patient will hold anything back from you. You know all about me now.'

'Ah. In that case it's time for diagnosis and treatment. Will you promise to follow my prescription faithfully, Lyn?'

The music came to an end. 'Probably not,' she said. 'I don't have all that much faith in doctors. Remember, I am one.' They walked back to their table.

The evening progressed, and she had a marvellous time. Other people came over to their table and asked her to dance. Edward Burrows, the saturnine consultant from Outpatients, came and waltzed with her and thanked her once more for rescuing baby Charlotte Jackson. A big pink medical student who had looked round the ward a couple of weeks ago invited her to jive. Although she wanted to spend time with Ross, she thought it an excellent idea that people weren't sticking to their own little groups, but were wandering round and chatting to others.

Ross had excused himself and gone table-hopping and, to her surprise, Sir Sidney asked her to dance. Even more to her surprise, he was good at it, moving with far more skill than his son.

'I like Ross McKinnon,' he said unexpectedly. 'Usually an SR who goes table-hopping will talk to other consultants, or even edge towards the hospital manager's table. This could be a night for networking. But not Ross, he's talking to friends. Who's that he's with now?'

There was Ross, sitting laughing with a small group. 'They're the ward cleaners,' Lyn said.

'Might have guessed.' They twirled round a couple more times and then he went on, 'I'm a heart surgeon, and I know that having a big heart means illness and probably an early death. But speaking for a moment poetically—Ross has a big heart.'

'I know,' said Lyn sincerely.

She was wondering how someone as open as Sir Sidney could have a reserved daughter like Melissa. It seemed strange. Simon was much more obviously Sir Sidney's son.

The evening went on. She danced with Ross, she danced with Simon, she danced with people who ambled over and asked her. At one stage Simon brought two bottles of champagne over, but after she had had a couple of glasses she returned to the iced lemon, which was much more refreshing. Then, when the evening was nearly over, a young nurse, still in her uniform of black trousers and white shirt, and with the pink epaulette that indicated that she was a student, came hurrying over to their table. She looked concerned.

It was Ross she wanted, and he smiled at her kindly, as he did to all the junior staff. She whispered something to him, he glanced at his watch and nodded. Then she darted away.

'Trouble?' Sir Sidney asked.

'Not really. The night sister on the ward is new and a bit nervous, and now she has a minor problem A temperature has spiked so she wondered about increasing the dosage. Henry's on call but she doesn't want to fetch him out unnecessarily. They know I'm in the building so asked if I could spare ten minutes.' He looked grim. 'She should be able to cope but…please excuse me, I'll be back as quickly as I can.' He walked towards the exit.

'Would you like to dance?' asked Simon.

Lyn shook her head. 'I'm really enjoying myself, but now the heat is getting to me.'

'It's affecting me, too. Would you like to walk to the foyer, have a breath of fresh air?'

When he said it, she realised that this was just what she wanted. She hesitated, then said, 'Well, just for a moment, then. Are you coming, Melissa?'

Melissa was now alone at the table. 'I'm fine, thanks,' she said. Lyn wondered at the odd expression on her face.

Simon led her through the foyer to the open air, and they sat on a bench just outside the great sheets of glass. He took her hand in his, and briskly she removed it. 'I've really enjoyed spending time with you, Lyn,' he said. 'I was wondering if we might—'

Then things fell into place.

'I'm going to tell you something about my private life,' she interrupted. 'Did you know I was engaged? My fiancé was killed in a climbing accident nine months ago.'

She could tell by his horrified expression that he didn't know. 'Lyn…I'm so sorry…no one told—'

She went on, 'This is the first time I've really been out, really enjoyed myself since it happened. It's been great, two gorgeous men vying for me. Every girl in the place has envied me, and I've had a wonderful time.' She paused. 'It's a pity that one of the two men was put up to it by his sister. You were supposed to divert me while Melissa concentrated on Ross, weren't you?'

He didn't speak. She looked at his bowed shoulders, his woebegone face, and realised that she quite liked him. 'Sorry, Lyn,' he said quietly. 'I didn't know about you. If I had, I wouldn't have done what Melissa wanted. She's helped me in the past with a couple of scrapes I've got into, so when she asked me to do this, I...'

'It was still a bit low,' Lyn said.

'I know it was.' He was silent a while longer, and then went on, 'You're not going to believe this. I don't believe it myself. You're right, I was supposed to make you fall for me. Anyway, I haven't succeeded, I've been found out in a mean little scheme and just the opposite has happened. Lyn, I think I've rather fallen for you.'

'Simon! You can't *still* be trying to con me!'

'I'm not. It's going to cause me to suffer, and, let's face it, I deserve it.' He thought a moment and said, 'I don't suppose there's any chance you'd have lunch with me some time?'

'No. I'm busy and there already is a man in my life— sort of.' She thought a minute. 'Simon, did your father know about this little plan of Melissa's?'

'No. It's not his style.' Simon frowned. 'But I wouldn't be surprised if he guessed. He's a wily old devil.'

'I like him,' Lyn said.

'So will you forgive me?'

'I guess so. After all, as I said, I've had two gorgeous men chasing me instead of one.'

'Truer than you think,' he muttered. 'Lyn, there's another thing. I've got no right to ask you this, but I will. Will you go easy on Melissa? She'd kill me if she knew I was telling you, but I'm going to. Melissa was adopted. My parents thought they couldn't have children. Then as often happens, I came along. Melissa couldn't have been loved more, but there's always been a bit of insecurity, and when our mother died five years ago it got worse.'

Lyn leaned over and kissed him on the cheek. 'I think she's very lucky having you as a brother. And don't worry, I'll not get upset. Now, let's get back to the dance.'

They arrived to find Sir Sidney, Melissa and Ross talking. Lyn caught the quick glance between Melissa and Simon, registered his sheepish expression. She wouldn't have been human if she hadn't taken some pleasure in the situation. She walked over to Ross. 'The evening's going to finish soon,' she said, 'but I'm still in the mood for dancing if you are.'

'Seize the day,' he said, and led her onto the floor.

Her words were prophetic, because before they started to dance there was the announcement—this must be the last waltz. She didn't have time to think about what she wanted to say next, or to consider the most appropriate way of putting it. She took a deep breath. 'It's been a wonderful evening,' she said. 'There's bound to be a fight for taxis and I'm tired. May I stay at your place tonight?'

There. She'd said it.

'Of course,' he said. 'The accommodation is a bit cramped, but you're welcome to what there is. Is this an immoral proposition, or do you merely want somewhere to sleep?'

She looked up. She knew he'd be smiling and he was.

'I'm tired,' she said. 'Who knows what tomorrow may bring? But for tonight I need a couch or an easy chair or a bit of the floor.'

'In that case, the last squeeze of my toothpaste shall be yours.'

They rejoined the group. Sir Sidney said that he had arranged for his Rolls to call, could he offer her a lift home?

'I've already arranged a lift,' she said, bending the truth slightly, 'but thank you anyway.'

'I know you're kept pretty busy, but if you ever want a look round my place I'd like to show you.'

It was an offer that pleased her. 'I'll certainly take you

up on that,' she said. She shook his hand, kissed him on the cheek, and then did the same to Simon.

She didn't want to crow over Melissa. So she shook her hand, and kissed her too. 'Being with a group, with you, your father and Simon, made the evening for me,' she said, with some degree of honesty. 'But it's back to work on Monday, and nothing will have changed.'

Melissa got the message. 'It never does,' she said. 'Thanks for everything, Lyn.'

The end of any fancy dress party was always half comic, half sad, Lyn thought as she watched the last of the costumed merry-makers trail out of the hall. Everyone knew that the party had ended, that real life had started again and it was strange to be dressed up as a fairy or a Roman soldier. There were a few jokes, a few comments, and then she and Ross were standing alone in the foyer.

Now she was nervous. She had started something, and she wasn't sure whether she wanted to go on. With his uncanny ability to recognise what she was feeling, he knew this.

He put his arm round her shoulders. 'This is London,' he said. 'There's always a taxi. You could be home in fifteen minutes.'

She was determined. 'No. I want to stay.'

'Then I live this way. We'll pick up your coat as we walk.'

She knew that the hospital had a block of modern flatlets that were let out to staff. But it was unusual for a specialist registrar to live in one. 'Why don't you buy a place of your own?' she asked curiously. 'You could easily afford to, you're not a poor student any more.'

He shrugged. 'Why do I need a house or a flat? I'm away whenever I can and this place is handy and no trouble. I don't want roots, I guess.'

'So this is all the home you have?'

'Not exactly. My brother is a GP in the wilds of Norfolk, and I keep a room in his house.'

'That was his boat we borrowed,' she said, interested. 'I can't think of there being another Ross McKinnon. Is he like you?'

He laughed. 'Peter? I suppose he is, in some way. But he's older, very happy in his job, has a lovely wife and four outrageous kids. He did better than your projected two-point-four children.'

'Quite,' she said.

'His wife is Angela, and she's always telling me it's time I settled down, that I should find a good woman and get married. I think she worries that I might be a bad influence on her husband. I might unsettle him.'

'It sounds like he has an ideal life. He won't be unsettled.' She decided not to comment about his search for a 'good woman'.

Walking through the cool night air had wakened her slightly, but as they reached the door to the flats she staggered a little. Instantly he reached to support her. 'I didn't think you were that drunk.' He grinned.

'Hardly. I've had a big, big wonderful evening, I worked till gone midnight last night, I've been all day preparing for this party—and, yes, I have had a drink. But, basically, I'm just dead beat.'

'We're nearly there.' With an arm round her, he escorted her up a flight of steps, and opened a door. 'Here. The McKinnon luxury penthouse flat.'

Now she was more weary than ever. She blinked. 'It looks like the inside of a toy box,' she said. There were assorted bits of furniture, and two walls of bookshelves. She sat heavily on the bed.

'Time for me to play the thoughtful host,' he said. From

a cupboard he took a towelling dressing gown, a thick
flannel shirt. He pulled her to her feet, and pointed her to
a door. 'Go and have a shower,' he said. 'There are clean
towels in the airing cupboard and toothbrushes in a box.
You can use this shirt as a nightgown; it's the biggest I've
got.'

She wondered what he was talking about, then with
unsteady legs made her way to the bathroom. She was
exhausted! Whatever else she had expected of the evening, it wasn't that she'd promptly want to fall to sleep.

It was a small but practical bathroom. She hung up her
dress, showered, removed her make-up and cleaned her
teeth. She felt a tiny touch more awake—but not much.
His shirt made a comfortable but revealing nightie, so she
pulled on the dressing gown and went back.

Apprehension was fighting with fatigue as she looked
at him. 'This wasn't quite what I had intended.' She
yawned, and he laughed.

'Bed,' he said. She looked at the single divan in the
corner of the room. It looked so attractive, with the top
turned down to show pale blue sheets under a tartan
throw. Then she saw a sleeping bag stretched out on the
rug.

'I'm not taking your bed,' she protested. 'I...'

'No arguments. I've spent nearly as much time in a
sleeping bag as I have in a bed.'

Well, so had she, and she knew which she preferred.
'When I said I wanted to stay with you...' she mumbled,
but he led her to the bed, sat her in it and handed her a
mug. She'd wondered what the nice smell was.

'Cocoa,' he said. 'Comfort for body and soul.'

She sipped, and looked at him in shock. 'Cocoa?' she
asked.

'Well, I added some brandy. Gives it a kick, don't you think?'

It certainly had some kind of effect. She drank most of it, then she was vaguely aware of someone taking the mug from her hands, easing off the dressing gown, and sliding her legs into the bed. She was so tired. Perhaps someone kissed her on the forehead. She didn't know. Perhaps it was a dream.

CHAPTER SEVEN

LYN knew where she was instantly when she awoke. She was in Ross's bed. Life felt good, she was happy in herself, waking more contented than she could remember in a very long time. Yesterday, last night, had been wonderful. Except the last few minutes? She hadn't intended to get so tired. But Ross hadn't seemed to mind. She was sure he hadn't minded. And perhaps she could make it up to him.

She turned, trying not to let the bed creak. The bedside clock told her it was nine o'clock; it was months since she'd slept as late as this. By the light through a crack in the curtains, she looked at Ross. He was lying on his side in the sleeping bag, with his back to her. An arm and a shoulder were out of the bag, and they were naked. She wondered if he was wearing anything at all.

Rooms told you about people, Lyn believed. This one had the normal, quite pleasant hospital furniture, the desk, bed, chairs and assorted cupboards. Ross had contributed the computer and lined two of the walls with bookshelves. They were untidy. There were piles of papers, magazines, and pictures among the books. She looked at the pictures.

One was of a smiling group in climbing kit, with a snow-capped mountain in the background. There were other mountain pictures, and a couple of a jungle-banked river. Only one picture didn't show mountains or rivers or great expanses of ice. It was a family picture, of a tall man who could only be Ross's brother, with a pretty blonde wife and four children. They all looked—contented.

Many of the books were familiar medical tomes, some less familiar. Ross evidently believed in keeping up with the latest developments. There was a surprising number of books on natural history, and, of course, no end of books on travel and exploration. She sighed, and felt a little dismayed. But it was what she would have expected. As she leaned forward, the bed creaked.

Ross rolled onto his back, his eyes flicked open and he was looking at her. His long hair was tousled, he needed a shave and when he smiled at her he looked ridiculously attractive.

'Did you sleep well?' he asked.

The reason she was sleeping in his room came back to her, and she said rather primly, 'It was good of you to let me stay.'

He laughed, and she blushed.

Still in the sleeping bag, he rolled forward to his feet, and then hopped into the bathroom. A minute later he was out again, this time wearing another dressing gown. 'The kitchen is outside,' he said. 'Don't move till I come back. Tea or coffee to meet the day?'

'Tea, please.'

No sooner was he out of the door than she leaped out of bed, and into the bathroom herself. A quick wash and...what could she wear? She should have thought this through. Putting on the party dress again just didn't seem right at breakfast-time. So she put on his shirt again, and scrambled back into his bed.

He returned with a tray, a large brown pot of tea and a stack of brown toast. 'There's marmalade or peanut butter,' he said. 'Now don't tell me you don't eat breakfast, you need your early morning blood sugar.'

'I eat breakfast,' she told him.

He put the tray on the bedside table, then sat on a cushion beside the bed. 'This *is* nice,' he told her. 'Breakfast is the best meal of the day, and it's so pleasant to share it with someone.'

She buttered a piece of toast. 'I'm sure you're right.' Her awkwardness was going, and now she did feel at home sitting with him, even if both of them were half naked. He made her relax, she decided.

'How am I going to get home?' she asked. 'It'll look a bit odd, wearing my party dress in the daytime.'

'No problem. I'll lend you a track suit and bring the Land Rover round to the front door. We'll smuggle you back to your flat easily.'

'Good.' Yes, she did feel relaxed. 'There's another thing I forgot to mention yesterday. My parents are home again. I checked the roster, and we're both free in a week. Fancy going down to see them?'

'That would be great!' His enthusiasm was obviously genuine. Then he asked with a sly grin, 'Will they see me as a prospective suitor?'

'No,' she said with a sigh. 'They'll see you as another lunatic climber and traveller.'

Contentedly, she drank some tea, and went on, 'I slept like a baby, because I was tired and I was happy. Last night was wonderful, Ross. It was a symbol for me, like coming out of darkness. I'm still going to work hard, but it won't be the only thing in my life—I'm going to enjoy myself too. I'm free of the past; I'm going to think of the future.'

'I'm glad.' He reached over and stroked her arm, before beginning to stroke elsewhere.

After a while, she giggled and said, 'I like your little

flat. But the bed's too small. Still, d'you think we could get two in it?'

He looked troubled. 'Lyn, are you sure…?'

'Yes, I'm sure.' She hesitated. 'Ross, have you…got something?'

He knew what she meant at once. 'I can take care of you, darling.'

She wriggled to the far side of the bed, then, in a semi-defiant gesture, sat up and pulled the shirt over her head. He slipped off his dressing gown and slid in beside her.

Instantly his arms were round her, his lips seeking hers. She revelled in the ardour of his kiss, the way he pulled her to him as if he could not control himself. She realised that unconsciously she had wanted this for so long! But then he slowed, moved his head from hers. She frowned; what was wrong?

'No hurry, no hurry,' he whispered. 'We have all the time in the world.'

They had been side by side, but now he eased her onto her back, leaned over her and kissed her again, but this time more gently. With his tongue he teased the sensitive corners of her eyes, her mouth, he bit the softness of her ear. He still hadn't shaved, and the roughness of his skin on hers excited her. 'No hurry,' he whispered again. 'No hurry.'

Now his lips were dipping further, kissing her neck, the soft slopes of her breasts, then finally the hard, excited peaks themselves. He took her into his mouth, and she sighed with ecstasy, arching her body against him. She twisted her hand in his hair, unable to bear the pleasure. 'Ross, oh, Ross,' she murmured huskily.

It was a small bed, so they were forced together, making her all too aware of his longing for her. He lifted his head to kiss her lips again, and, knowing what he wanted—what they both wanted—she pulled him onto her, opening herself to him. It felt so good! Then there was that moment, half of anticipation, half of fear, and they were together. She could feel his excitement; it thrilled her and she lifted herself to hold him.

For a while she revelled in taking and giving pleasure, in the rhythm that they created together. Then she felt his increased urgency, and pulled him harder to her as their frenzy mounted, then joined together with him in a half-screamed climax.

He lay, his head on her shoulder, and she could feel the rapid thudding of his heart. She could feel the beat of her own heart. 'I love you,' he said.

Later he fetched more tea, and they sat in bed and talked. Then she pulled on his shirt again—she was still too modest to stay entirely naked—and walked round his room, looking at books, asking about pictures. There was so much she wanted to know about him. She opened drawers and looked at his ties, peered in the cupboards where his suits hung.

'This is your brother, isn't it?' she asked, looking at the family picture.

'That's Peter and Angela and the brood. I'll take you to see them all, when we have time. Angela will look at me meaningfully.'

'They look a happy family, I'd like to meet them. Who's this? Oh, you're standing next to that broadcaster!'

It was the picture of the climbers, with the background of the snowy mountain range. 'That's in the Himalayas. Taken about five years ago. There was a television crew waiting for us at base camp.'

'So that's why the broadcaster. And who's this next to you? He looks nice.'

'Brian Lendall.'

Something about his voice made her look up. 'Go on. Tell me.'

'He was killed on an expedition two years later.'

She couldn't stop herself asking. 'Did he have a family?'

'A wife. Two children.'

She decided to talk about something else at once. 'If you want to take me home I'll invite you to lunch.'

'I'd like that. But your bed's even smaller than mine.'

'You only want me for one thing,' she told him cheekily. 'Mind you, it's something I like too.'

He lent her an old track suit. In it she looked ludicrous—the legs were far too long and she was lost in the top. Fortunately there weren't too many people around. He fetched the Land Rover and, dress over her arm, she warily scampered down the stairs.

Things were different now. Last time he'd been in her flat she'd been on edge, not sure of what to make of him, not sure where their relationship had been going. Now things were easier. He sprawled on her bed as she dressed in her own clothes. Then, just as she had done, he wandered round the room, opening drawers, peering in cupboards.

'These won't keep you very warm.' He grinned, pulling open her underwear drawer.

'They're not meant to. They're meant to look nice, and make me feel nice. I like dressing well.'

'I've noticed,' he said.

She cooked him a huge, high-cholesterol brunch: ham, eggs, sausages, tomatoes and mushrooms.

'Where's the black pudding?' he asked. 'That'll make this meal truly disgraceful and enjoyable.'

She tried to rap his knuckles with her spoon, but he

moved. 'I grilled everything,' she protested. 'Anyway, a bit of self-indulgence occasionally is good for you.'

'I think a bit of self-indulgence often is very good for me,' he told her, and she blushed.

'I was wondering if you might like to—' she started.

His mobile phone rang. They looked at each other sadly. 'I started on call at one o'clock,' he said. 'Yes? Ross McKinnon here…'

It wasn't a great emergency but he said he would be at the hospital in an hour. 'Sit by me on the couch,' she said, 'and we'll have our coffee there.'

She rested her head on his shoulder, his arm round her waist. 'Meeting you and last night and this morning have changed my life,' she said. 'But I'm working hard and I'm enjoying it, so I don't want to make plans. When…when Gavin died, the best bit of advice I got was just to get through one day at a time. So I'm going to do that. When I met you I knew that something like this was going to happen. So I'm going to enjoy it. I'm going to seize the day.'

'Seize it with me,' he said. 'I think I've found something too.'

Her plans were shaken three days later.

It was half-past seven in the evening, she was in her flat changing out of her formal clothes into trousers and sweater. There was Frank Sinatra quietly singing 'Songs for Swingin' Lovers' on her player, and she felt at ease with the world.

She heard a key in the door of the flat. It turned, and she heard the door open. No one had a key to her flat!

Frightened, she looked down her hall. 'Who's there?' she quavered.

Her fright turned into terror. There was a dim figure

appearing through the door, tall, slim, blond. Just like Gavin, her fiancé who was dead! The figure moved into the light and she still had difficulty in believing what she saw. It was Doug, Gavin's older brother. They looked so much alike.

'You scared me!' she shouted. 'You really scared me. Doug, why didn't you phone or something?'

'Never thought to,' he muttered. 'Didn't think it necessary.' He walked further into the hall, and dumped the big rucksack he was carrying over one shoulder. He looked weary. Her shock now over, she moved forward to put her arms round him and hug him. He kissed her. He was wearing an old oiled canvas jacket, with that smell of rock and earth that she knew so well. She hadn't seen him for months because he had stayed in Borneo.

'Just got back this afternoon,' he told her. 'I'm bushed. There's a lot I've got to tell you, but for now I'll stay in my old place. Don't worry about bedding, I've got my sleeping bag here. Could you rustle up something for me to eat?'

She didn't know what to say. Then, 'Go and have a bath,' she said. 'I'll see what's in the freezer.'

Her first reaction was to phone Ross. She needed help with this; she just didn't know how to tackle it. After so long she thought she had finally got rid of Gavin's ghost. And now here was his brother, bringing back memories that she didn't want, reminding her of a lifestyle that she needed to forget. She had moved on. It looked as if Doug hadn't.

She found soup and a pizza in the freezer, set them to warm and sat down to think. First she had to face an unwelcome truth. She didn't want Doug here. But it looked as if she was stuck with him.

This was the way their group had lived. There had always been someone passing through, needing a bed for the night—or, more usually, a place to spread their sleeping bag. It had been like a freemasonry, and she herself had slept on the floor of comparative strangers in Wales and the Lake District.

Doug had qualified as a doctor, but he had never followed the profession seriously. He would work for a few months to gather some money, then disappear to a distant part of the world until his money ran out. He would turn up unannounced, and sleep in the roof space which now she used as a store. It looked as if he didn't realise that things had changed. She wasn't looking forward to telling him.

When he was sitting opposite her at the kitchen table, she felt a little differently. He was thinner than she remembered. There was a new scar on his forehead and, instead of laughing so much as he used to, he looked very serious. She fetched him a beer.

'I'll hang around a week or two, and then get some agency work,' he told her. 'I need to get some money together. But I fancy staying in London for a while. Got fed up with Borneo.'

'How did you get that scar on your forehead?' she asked.

He laughed, and drained the bottle. 'Is there another beer?' he asked. Then, 'I fell off the same rock face that Gavin was killed on. I thought I owed it to him to finish the climb so I went back to have another go. But it was harder than I thought. It was harder than both of us thought. Had to spend a couple of months recuperating.'

I don't need this, she thought wildly to herself. I've finished with this macho, fight-everything attitude. I've got a new life. But she said nothing to Doug. She knew he would only look at her uncomprehendingly. And she wished he didn't look so much like Gavin. Gavin was dead!

He might have been reading her mind. 'It was a good climb,' he told her—as if it mattered! 'Gav wanted to solo it, which was a bit of a daft thing to do. But you know what he was like. Anyway he peeled, dropped and I got to him. Nothing to be done for him. But he was still alive, and he was thinking of you. Made me promise to look after you. So I'm here, and that's what I'm going to do.'

Now the tears were running down her face. She knew everything Doug had said was accurate; it all was so dreadfully true to life. 'You could have written and told me,' she said. 'I would have liked a letter, it would have...helped.'

Doug looked surprised. 'I don't like writing much,' he said.

He stood, and stretched. 'Think I'll turn in,' he said. 'You'll be working tomorrow, so don't worry about me, I'll sort myself out. But tomorrow night I'll take you out to dinner. Remember that Indian restaurant we used to go to, where they serve that super hot curry?'

She remembered it. She didn't like it. Acidly she said, 'I see no point in eating a curry so hot you can taste nothing. It doesn't sound like much of a test of your manhood to me. It never did.'

He ignored her comment. 'I haven't had a good hot curry in months.'

She remembered something. 'Anyway, I can't go out with you. I'm already meeting someone.' Ross had invited her to a quick supper at a local pub, and she was looking forward to it.

'Who're you going out with? Is he more important than me?'

The questions were snapped out, and she was surprised

at the anger in his voice. At first she was going to tell him it was none of his business—but then, they were old friends. 'Just someone I work with,' she said placatingly. 'We've got business to talk about.'

'Put him off. Tell him to keep business for when you're at work.' Then there was a complete change of tone as he leaned over her and kissed her cheek. 'Goodnight, Lyn. It's been so good to see you again. Things are going to be the same as before, don't worry. I'll see to it.'

She sat at the kitchen table, hearing the rumble of the ladder being pulled down. He'd leave it down, she knew. She wished she could push up the ladder, and push him out of her life again. And then she felt guilty. They'd been close. Hadn't they?

'I've got a lodger,' she told Ross on the telephone next day. 'Not exactly expected, but what can I do?' She told him about Doug's unexpected arrival, about the kind of life they had used to lead, about not being able to get out to meet him that night.

'You've got problems,' Ross said sympathetically. 'Lyn, I know—well, I can guess at—what the fellow used to mean to you. But times have moved on. D'you think you're being entirely wise, letting him dictate to you?'

She had wondered about this herself. But... 'I don't think meeting you just yet is a good idea,' she said. 'He's my fiancé's brother, and I know he'd do anything for me. He's still jet-lagged, still not come to terms with things. It'll all sort itself out.'

'For your sake, I hope so. Enjoy your meal tonight, I wish you were with me. Love you.'

Not a very satisfactory phone call, she thought as she rang off. Ross had only said what she already thought. She wasn't being very wise. She remembered the way

Doug and Gavin had used to order her life, making her decisions for her. In retrospect, she hadn't liked it. But she'd been in love, so would have done anything for her lover.

She wasn't in love now. The thought shocked her, and then she worked out what she meant by it. She *was* in love, but she was in love with Ross. She just wasn't in love with Gavin now.

The meal wasn't a success. Doug ordered the hottest curry as she knew he would, and tried to make her do the same. When she refused, he looked quite sulky. To cool his mouth he ordered a pitcher of lager, and had two more before the meal was finished. The alcohol made him slightly maudlin. He told her again about how Gavin died, and that he was here to look after her. Altogether, not a good evening.

'We could go out somewhere on Sunday,' he said when they got back to the flat. 'Go for a walk somewhere.'

She was taking Ross to see her parents, but she wasn't going to tell Doug this. 'I'll have to put a day in at the hospital,' she said. 'Sorry, Doug.'

'You work too hard! I'll have to see what I can do about it.'

She watched as he climbed the ladder to his bed. She had no fears of him falling. Drunk or sober, Doug could climb anything. Almost.

'I shall muss you, Dr Lyn,' Fatima said proudly.

Lyn turned to beam at her. This was a sentence obviously memorised carefully; Fatima's English was still fairly non-existent. 'I shall miss you too,' she said, and tried again one of her own memorised Arabic sentences. Her Arabic must be getting better—Fatima didn't laugh.

There was no one for Fatima to play with on the ward,

and no one to talk to either. So Lyn had got into the habit of taking her down to the foyer every morning, where they had a coffee and an orange juice. She thought that the two of them were becoming friends. But the next day Fatima was to be discharged, and her father would come to pick her up.

'I hope I see you again some time,' Lyn continued, holding out her hand to the little girl. 'It won't be the same without you.'

Fatima took the outstretched hand, and the two of them set off back. 'Thank you, Dr Lyn,' Fatima said.

Ross had wanted to pick her up at her flat on Sunday morning but she had persuaded him not to. 'I'll take a taxi down to the hospital,' she told him. 'My flat isn't on the route we're going to take.

He knew why she didn't want him to call. 'You're worried about what Doug will think if I turn up, aren't you?' he asked. 'Lyn, this is not a good idea. I love you, you love me, even if you haven't said so we should live for each other, but Doug is taking over your life.'

'It's just for a while. And I feel all sorts of mixed emotions. I couldn't throw him out, there's too much of my past wrapped up in him.'

'Was it a happy past?'

That was a good question. She was beginning to rethink things. With difficulty she said, 'I thought I was—no, I knew I was in love with Gavin. But now I'm wondering if that love would have lasted.'

He put his arm round her, and squeezed her. 'This is something I can't help with,' he said. 'I'm prejudiced. Just remember how much you mean to me.'

Once again they had an early start. As she stepped out of the taxi, at the front of the hospital, he was waiting for her in the Land Rover. She climbed up into the front seat, leaned over to kiss him, then said, 'Let's go.' She looked at the back seat. 'Flowers,' she remarked, then, 'What's in the bag?'

'A surprise. I'll show you later.'

She might have guessed he would be a good navigator. He drove through the light early morning traffic and soon they were on the M4 heading west. At first there were the interminable suburbs, but soon enough they were driving through green fields, with the sight of birds, and the line of downs in the distance.

'I thought I was a town girl now,' she said thoughtfully. 'But when I see a bit of greenery, I realise what I'm missing.'

'I know what you mean. Now, tell me what your parents are like. I think I know them from their books, but I'd like to know more about them before we meet.'

'You sound like the anxious suitor.' She giggled. 'But I don't think they will ask you what your intentions are. They'll approve of the outfit, though.'

He did look well. A grey leather coat over a thin burgundy sweater, cavalry twill trousers and stout shoes made him look ready for a day in the country.

'One does one's best,' he said. 'Now, I've bought flowers for your mother. But I need to know more.'

'Right. When they're in England they live in an old farmhouse, Woodend Grange. It used to be my grandmother's. The farm has been in the family for generations, and she always hoped that my father would run it. But he had the wandering bug, and the farm is let out to a local farmer.'

'You lived there with your grandmother? You said once that you stayed with her in term time so you could study?'

'Yes. She insisted I had regular schooling, and sympathised when I told her I wanted to be a doctor. She died just over a year ago, and I was so glad that she'd seen me qualify. She wasn't so very old and her death hit me hard. In fact...'

'You've thought of something?' he asked gently, when she didn't finish her sentence.

'I can't believe it,' she said. 'It's just not possible.'

'Tell me. I'll say if it's possible or not.'

She shook her head, bewildered. 'I don't know what to think. It just struck me. My grandmother had died, I was very upset and working far too hard, my parents were away on the far side of the world. And I got engaged.'

Delicately, he asked, 'You think you might have—got engaged for the wrong reasons?'

'I think so.' She paused, and then said, 'Ross, I feel terrible. I feel disloyal to my dead fiancé. He *loved* me. And I loved him.'

'Love takes many different forms,' he told her. 'Who can tell which is the most real?'

'I don't know what to say. Can we have some music on, please?' She felt very mixed up and tearful, and it showed in her voice.

He said nothing, but selected a tape and slid it into the player. He'd chosen Vivaldi's 'Four Seasons'. As the cheerful birdsong of 'Spring' filled the car, she started to feel better. She might have made mistakes in her past, but she would be careful not to make them again.

They bypassed Bristol, crossed the Severn Bridge, and turned right onto the A48. Her heart was beating a little faster now. This land always meant going home to her. It was so beautiful, in the softer, very English way of the Forest of Dean. She recognised villages, houses of old friends, walks she had undertaken when young. Then they were driving up to Woodend Grange, the only place she had ever really thought of as home. They passed along the drive, through the slightly neglected garden, and she saw the old grey stone building ahead.

The Land Rover crunched to a stop on the gravel outside the front door. Her parents must have been listening for them, for they came promptly out onto the front step. Lyn's heart leaped when she saw them; she sometimes forgot just how much she loved them. Both were in their mid-fifties, both had greying hair, but their bodies moved with the grace and assurance of a fit twenty-year-old.

Gloomily, she saw them exchange a look of approval when they saw the Land Rover. She had known they would like it. She jumped down, hugged and kissed them both, then turned and said, 'Ma, Pa, this is Ross McKinnon. I work with him, and he wanted to meet you.'

'Really pleased to meet you, Ross,' said her father, extending a hand. 'Come and have a drink and then we'll go for a walk before lunch.'

Ross got on well, too well, with her parents, she thought sadly. Her mother was pleased with the flowers he had brought; both her parents were pleased with the contents of the bag on the back seat. Ross owned all her parents' books, and he had brought them all to be signed. Even better, the books showed signs of being read and re-read. Ross was going to be made very welcome.

First they had a quick cup of tea and then they went for a walk. After being cooped up in the car it was a real pleasure, and there were bitter-sweet memories of her childhood to point out. 'I must come here more often,' she said to Ross. 'I forget how much I love it.'

'I don't know how you can stay away. This is a glorious place; I'd like to stay here for ever.'

'Except when you were travelling to somewhere wild abroad,' she reminded him.

'Except then,' he agreed, urbanely.

Their projected short walk turned into a longer one, as it so often did. But eventually they got back to the farm-house. Ross had already mentioned his interest in the highlands of Peru. 'Come into the study, Ross, and I'll show you a few slides,' Lyn's father urged. 'Lyn and Jo can have a chat and carry on making lunch.'

Lyn looked at the two balefully. 'Don't think we're separating men's work from women's work,' she told Ross. 'After we've eaten, it'll be your turn to wash up.'

'No problem, I'll be happy to.'

She sighed. She knew he meant it.

They ate in the conservatory her father had built onto the side of the house. Her parent liked eating as close to the open air as possible. As ever the meal was simple, mostly home-grown produce from local farms. Once again this was a habit learned abroad; her parents were accus-tomed to buying their food in the tiny local markets.

'We know something of this American outfit that may offer Ross a job,' Jack Webster said when they were all seated round the old oak table. 'We met a party of them somewhere up the Amazon, and they were thinking of setting up a hospital there too.'

'Did they seem efficient?' asked Ross. 'Did they know what they were doing?'

'I would say very much yes. They weren't emphasising the religious bit and they weren't looking for converts. At least, not yet. They had some good local people working with them and they'd listen to advice. They struck me as being hard-headed. They had ample funds, but they didn't think that every problem could be solved by throwing money at it.'

'I found that with an American mission in the Himalayas,' Ross agreed. 'They were well supported, but they weren't going to waste a penny. I liked them for it.'

He went on to tell them what he knew about the plan for Peru. Lyn listened with sinking heart.

'If I take the job I know it'll keep me pretty busy,' Ross enthused, 'but not a hundred miles away there's this range called the Grey Mountains. As far as I can find out no one has ever explored them properly. Certainly there are peaks there that have never been climbed. I intend to find time to get over there.'

'Sounds great,' Jo said. 'We've been on the other side—the headwaters of the Amazon—but never climbed into the Andes from Peru.'

'Come and stay,' Ross said promptly. 'Once I'm firmly established I'll write, and perhaps we can organise something together.'

'They need doctors up there,' Jack said thoughtfully. 'Or at least some training. I remember when we were in the Amazon, one of the local tribes brought a child to our camp. She was ill, the symptom was a pain in the belly. Well, I'd done a First Aid course, and I knew quite a bit about common jungle diseases—we always carried extra medicines for anyone who might need them. But this was something new to me. So I looked up the medical book that we always carried, and worked out what was wrong. Appendicitis. In fact the book gave detailed instructions on how to take an appendix out, but I didn't dare. So we canoed back downstream and tried to get the child to the nearest hospital. But the appendix ruptured, and the child died of peritonitis.'

'Not a difficult operation, an appendectomy,' Lyn said. 'Any doctor could do one in an emergency.'

She felt rather left out in the excited planning that was

taking place. When the dishes were removed from the table Jack fetched the big-scale maps of the area, and he, Jo and Ross bent over them eagerly.

'Don't worry, I'll wash up,' Lyn said, half sarcastically. Her sarcasm didn't work.

'That's nice of you, dear,' her mother said abstractedly. 'Now, Ross, this river here…'

In fact it was Ross who straightened and offered to help, but Lyn had decided to be a martyr. 'It doesn't matter,' she assured him. 'You stay here and plan. You came to meet my parents, and I want you to talk to them.'

She went to the kitchen not in a tremendously good mood, but two minutes later her mother came to help. 'I do like him,' she said, seizing a drying cloth. 'Very interesting to talk to, and quite good-looking. Do you see a lot of him?'

'Not a lot. He's on my firm, but much of the time he's working at a different hospital.'

'He seems to think a lot of you. D'you think you've got over Gavin now? It is quite a while ago.'

'Yes, I've got over Gavin,' Lyn snapped. 'But I'm too busy to look for a replacement. And I certainly don't want another man whose idea of a good time is to travel to somewhere God-forsaken and leave me at home.' She couldn't tell her mother she was falling in love with the wrong man again.

'I liked Gavin,' her mother said inconsequentially, 'but I like Ross more. He's got much more sense, dear.'

'Much more sense,' Lyn muttered to herself. 'Of course he has. I wish I was the same.' Out loud she asked, 'Should I make coffee for us all?'

The rest of the afternoon passed more or less pleasantly. Eventually Lyn found herself drawn into the general enthusiasm, for she had forgotten how much fun planning a trip could be. Ross and her parents got on famously, and she couldn't remember them taking to someone so quickly. But eventually it was time to go, as they knew the traffic on the way back would be heavy.

'Get Lyn to bring you again soon,' her father called, 'or drop in yourself. You know where we live now.'

Her mother kissed her, and then kissed Ross. 'Been lovely to see you, Ross. Don't lose touch, we want to know how things go.'

Then they were on their way. One last wave, one last sad glimpse of the old grey building and they were driving back to London. Lyn didn't know how she felt. Her feelings were mixed. 'I'll drive some of the way if you like,' she said abruptly.

'I'd appreciate that. Take over when we get on the motorway?' His easy acquiescence irritated her even more.

'I really liked your parents,' he said when she had taken the wheel. 'They were all I had expected, and more besides.'

'They liked you, too. You're just the sort of man they hoped their daughter would bring home.' She knew her voice was cold.

He noticed too. 'What's the matter, Lyn? Why are you irritated? Something I said?'

'I'm glad they liked you. You said nothing that you haven't said before. You didn't need to go out of your way to charm them, you're just the kind of man they like. They liked Gavin, too.'

'Come on,' he said gently, 'we haven't known each other for long, but we don't want to fall out over a simple misunderstanding. Tell me what's wrong and if I can I'll put it right.'

'You can't put it right. It's what you are. I am very…attracted to you. But I'm not going to have a relationship with another Gavin. Not a serious relationship, anyway. The Gavins of this world just won't be tied down. That's fair enough, they know what they want. But equally, I'm not going to be left behind while the man in my life wanders off into the wilderness and risks coming home in a…in a metal box. They sent me Gavin's ashes, Ross, and I went and scattered them on a mountain top in Wales. I'm not going through that again.'

'All life is a risk,' he told her bleakly. 'You just have to face up to it.'

'Life *is* a risk. So why try to turn it into a bigger one?'

When he didn't answer she felt her anger disappearing. 'I'm sorry, I didn't want to upset you,' she said in a more reasonable tone. 'I was so glad that you got on with my parents, and I did enjoy visiting them with you. I was even proud of you! But the sight of you busy planning…it reminded me of times in the past. Times when I was left behind.'

His coldness disappeared too. 'Lyn, I said we haven't known each other very long. I'm thirty-two now. Of course, I've had relationships before, some of them quite serious. But I've never felt about anyone the way I feel about you. It happened so quickly, the first time we met. I thought it ridiculous! But we've got to give things time.'

'I'll get dragged in! I'll get hurt again!' she wailed.

'You know I would never do anything to hurt you!'

'You mean you would never deliberately do anything to hurt me.'

He bowed his head, acknowledging the fairness of what she said. 'We've both got work to do,' he said. 'Perhaps we haven't time to sort out complicated personal problems. Let's just recognise the problems are there, but carry on seeing each other. Quite often things sort themselves out.'

She paused before answering. 'You've made me happier than I've been for…years, I think. I couldn't bear not to see you. We'll do as you say. And if it turns out to be a relationship that's going nowhere—well, I will have been happy once.'

'That will do for now. We're friends. Dinner with me Tuesday night?'

'Looking forward to it already.'

He pulled loose his safety belt, and leaned over to kiss the side of her face. 'Careful,' she squeaked. 'Don't interfere with the driver.'

Things were settled. For the moment.

CHAPTER EIGHT

'I PHONED the hospital, this afternoon,' Doug said, 'and got through to your ward. They said you hadn't been in, that you had the day off.'

Lyn didn't need this. It had been a long, hard day, Ross had insisted on driving her home and she knew he'd been upset when she'd explained why she wouldn't invite him in for coffee.

'Lyn, I'm the man in your life now,' he had said. 'Now let's go upstairs together and introduce me to Doug. It's time we met!' Somehow she had persuaded him that it wasn't a good idea. But it had been hard.

'So where have you been?' Doug asked.

She turned on him in a fury. 'Don't you ever dare phone asking about me again. Whatever I do with my time is my affair and mine only. I've been to see my parents with Ross McKinnon, a man I work with, and whom I very much like.'

'You very much like? You can't very much like another man. What about Gavin?'

'Gavin is *dead*, Doug. You should know, you were there when he died. But life goes on. And if I find a man I like, then I'll go out with him.'

Suddenly she felt ashamed of herself. Doug's face was stricken, as if he couldn't comprehend what she was saying. There was shock in his eyes, dismay in the way his body went rigid. 'But…it's not a year yet,' he mumbled.

'I'm not getting engaged or anything, Doug. I'm just seeing him.' She thought of the conversation she had had

with Ross earlier, and said, 'We had a long talk on the
way home. I'm not sure how much longer we'll be seeing
each other. He's talking about going away for a couple
of years.'

She wasn't sure why she told Doug this; it was none
of his business. Perhaps because the conversation earlier
had been so hurtful. 'Now I'm having a bath and then I'm
going to bed.'

'Sorry about everything,' Doug said. 'I know I'm a bit
of a pain at times. I'll try to be better.' He smiled at her.
For a moment it was as if Gavin were in front of her, the
blond hair and tall, slumped figure reminded her so of
him. And that cheeky, little-boy smile, that was how he'd
always used to get round her. On impulse she went over,
hugged Doug and then kissed him. 'I'm not really angry,'
she said.

Before they had parted on Sunday Ross had suggested that
their Tuesday dinner date be at a new bistro he'd heard
about. 'It's rather posh,' he had said. 'Let's wear our interview suits.'

She had been rather excited by this, and on Monday
lunch-time managed to sneak out to a local boutique and
buy herself a new dress. It was red, emphasising her
curves, and the shop assistant said that it went well with
madam's hair. Well, of course it did.

Then early on Tuesday evening, when she got home
looking forward to a couple of hours' luxurious getting
ready, Doug said, 'There was a call for you five minutes
ago. A man called Ross McKinnon phoned and said he's
madly busy. He just can't get away tonight, he's got an
aneurism. Said not to call him, he's on the ward and he'll
ring when he has time.'

Lyn sighed, disappointed. But these things happened. 'I bought a new dress,' she complained.

'Then I'll take you out. Tell you what, I know you didn't like the Indian restaurant, *you* pick where we should go.'

She wanted to go out; she'd been looking forward to it. 'All right,' she said. 'There's a new steak and salad bar opened down the road. We'll try that.'

'Suits me. Going to wear your new dress?'

'No,' she said.

In fact the evening was quite pleasant. Doug snapped out of his morose mood and became again the good companion she remembered. They talked a little about old times but they did not dwell too much on the past. She enjoyed herself. But she'd rather have been with Ross. Ross was to Doug as claret was to beer.

On Wednesday evening things went downhill rapidly.

'Doug! I put those pictures away because I didn't ever want to see them again!' She couldn't believe what he had done.

Doug looked up from where he was stacking books in her bookshelf, and said curtly, 'This place has no character. We want it back the way it used to be.' He continued taking her textbooks out of the bookcase and replacing them with old climbing guides, dog-eared maps from long-past trips.

She looked around in increasing horror. It had been a hard day, and now she was home to find Doug had rearranged her living room. Her books were in piles, there were the old pictures on the walls, even ornaments, mementoes of days she wanted to forget. There was a slab of dolomite rock. A stuffed monkey she had always hated. This was stuff she should have thrown away!

'Doug! This is my flat! You're welcome to stay—for a while—but you don't live here and you don't rearrange things without my say-so. I've got the place how I like it, and that's the way it's going to be.'

She pulled a picture from the wall, grimacing as the pin tore out of the plaster.

Angrily Doug dragged the picture from her. 'That was taken on the top of the Eiger! It brings back memories. I want it where I can see it.'

'And I don't! Listen to me, Doug. This is *my* flat, I decide on the decorations. Right?'

Now he was really angry. 'What's wrong with you? The three of us were happy here, we had good times, we're going to have those good times again. But not with the place decorated like this!'

He picked up the fallen pin, hammered it back in the plaster and rehung the picture.

She couldn't believe her ears. 'Gavin is dead, Doug, d'you hear? He's dead! We have to move on. We aren't three any more, we're two. And you're only staying till you find somewhere else.'

'I know Gavin is dead! I was there when he died. You told me on Sunday night—you didn't need to, I already knew.'

As she watched he carefully straightened the picture. Then, with bewildering speed, his mood changed. He became conciliatory. 'Please, Lyn, can't we leave them here? Till we get things sorted out. Tell you what, just leave a couple of the pictures up and I'll put the rest away.'

She was tired, so she gave in. 'All right. You can leave just two pictures up. But they don't stay there for long.'

'Sure, not for long. I'm sorry, Lyn, I didn't mean to upset you.' He came over and hugged her, something he had done a lot recently. 'There were three of us, now there are only two of us. We can carry on as we used to. I'll take Gavin's place.' He kissed her.

She pushed him away, looking at him wide-eyed. 'What d'you mean, you'll take Gavin's place?'

'You've been working hard, you're tired,' he said. 'I'll go and make you a cup of tea.'

She watched him walk to the kitchen, unwilling even to think about what he had said. He'd take Gavin's place. The man must be mad!

She bathed and then changed, and when she came back into the living room he'd done as he'd said. Most of the pictures, the books and ornaments were gone. Just two mountain scenes remained, discreet and well placed. She had work to do that evening, and he was quiet and considerate, going to bed with a soft 'goodnight' well before she did. She put the earlier ugly scene out of her mind. She had other things to think about.

Next morning she was about to rush off to work when he called out, cheerfully, 'Lyn, it's awfully cramped up there in the attic. All right if I move down into the spare bedroom? Don't worry about shifting anything, I'll see to it all.'

She needed to leave at once; she didn't want to think or talk. 'I'm not sure that's a good idea. We don't need any more changes really, do we? You won't be here much longer. Look, we'll talk about it when I get back.'

She'd forgotten about the matter when she came home. Ross hadn't phoned, and she'd rather hoped he would. Of course, she could phone him—but he had cancelled their evening, and she felt it was up to him to phone first. Perhaps after their long talk on Sunday he'd decided to let their relationship cool. Did he think it wasn't going to go anywhere? Or perhaps he was still busy. Who could tell?

Doug had prepared tea, not a meal she would have picked, but she was grateful, because she felt too tired to cook. Afterwards she dozed in front of the television and tried to read a textbook. No good. She decided to go to bed early—and was surprised to see Doug coming out of the spare bedroom.

'What are you doing in there?' she asked crossly.

He looked genuinely perplexed. 'I've moved down. You remember, I asked you this morning.'

'But I didn't say yes. Doug…oh, what does it matter? Incidentally, you've been here a while now, isn't it time you started getting yourself sorted out? A job would be a good start.'

'Sorry about moving down when you didn't want me to,' he muttered. 'I'll move back tomorrow.'

'It doesn't matter! I'm going to bed. Stay where you are.'

She didn't sleep.

She came home early the next night. Work—or life—was getting on top of her, and she wasn't going to stay a minute longer than was necessary. She walked into the living room and there was Doug on the phone. He looked up, startled, as she entered the room and muttered down the phone, 'Sorry, I'll have to go.'

'Who rang?' she asked curiously. 'You haven't had a call before—no one knows you're here.'

'Doing what you said, trying to find a job. I'm looking for some agency work.'

'Should be easy enough to find in London,' she commented. 'They're really short.'

'You look worn out,' he said. 'Sit there and take it easy and I'll put the kettle on. A cup of tea'll fix you up.'

She sat in her favourite armchair, kicked off her shoes, and closed her eyes. And the minute she heard the kitchen door close she took the phone and dialled 1471. The courteous voice read out the last number to call. It was Ross's number. She rang him at once. His voice was cool.

'Please can we meet in the Mayflower tonight?' she asked. 'I've got a lot to tell you and to ask you.'

'You want to tell and ask yourself, not get your boyfriend to do it?'

'If I have a boyfriend—which I'm beginning to doubt—it's you. I haven't asked anyone to take or send messages for me.'

There was a pause, then, 'Ah,' he said. 'I think I see. Lyn, I've been stupid, I'm so sorry. When I rang and—'

'The Mayflower at half-past nine tonight,' she interrupted. 'We can talk then. That all right?'

'Fine.' He rang off.

Now it was Doug's turn to be suspicious. He placed the tea tray on the table between them and asked, 'Who was that on the phone?'

She didn't tell him to mind his own business. 'They want me back at work,' she said. 'I'm on call, I'll drop in for an hour after tea.'

'That place works you too hard! You should be at home looking after me.'

'It's what I'm paid for,' she said. She didn't want a fight. Not yet.

Over the next couple of hours she thought about confronting Doug. But she decided not to, not yet. First she wanted to talk to Ross. Something he had once said to her on the ward came back to her. 'Get all the facts before making a decision or a diagnosis. You can't decide on anything until you know everything.' Doug said little all evening, sitting in an armchair, reading.

At nine she told him she was going out, then walked down to the main road and hailed a taxi. She didn't want to travel by underground, she needed some peace. There were things she needed to work out.

The Mayflower was quiet and she saw Ross sitting in the same corner they'd sat in before. He looked worried. When he saw her approaching he stood, his smile apprehensive.

'I want a hug,' she said, and opened her arms. She didn't care where they were. It was so good to feel the strength of him, to be crushed against his hard chest, to smell his faint, lemony aftershave. Then they sat side by side in the banquette.

'Listen,' she said, 'on Sunday you said that whatever happened we could work things out. I should have remembered that. I misjudged you, I'm sorry.'

He shook his head. 'No, I was stupid. I should have known that kind of behaviour just wasn't you.'

She leaned up to kiss his cheek and said, 'I need a drink and I think I'd like a whisky. A double, in fact. Then we can talk like civilised human beings who...'

'Who love each other?' he suggested.

'Yes, who love each other. I think talking is part of loving.'

He fetched her whisky, and brought the same for himself. 'I'll talk first,' he said. 'Your turn next. I was worried after Sunday. I knew we had differences, but I hoped we could work them out. I was very much looking forward to Tuesday.'

She couldn't restrain herself. 'So was I,' she said. 'I bought a new dress.'

He smiled. 'When I phoned you early on Tuesday evening, a very reasonable-sounding man answered—presumably Doug. He apologised and said he'd been asked to give me a message. You didn't want to come out to dinner. You were thinking about the relationship, and needed time to work out what was best. And please, I wasn't to try to get in touch. Doug was very apologetic, and said he was very sorry but that was it.'

Anger flared in her. 'I never said any of that!'

'I know. I should have known—but he was so plausible. I decided to ignore what I thought you'd said, and phoned again tonight. He was pleasant again and still plausible. Then you rang, and it all came together.'

'He tricked us both,' she said slowly. 'And I never doubted him once.'

'He's very, very clever,' Ross said. 'You should recognise this kind of manipulative behaviour, Lyn. The man has no conscience. He's a sociopath.'

At first she was ready to disagree. Then she thought. 'I do recognise this kind of behaviour,' she said slowly. 'I recognise it, I remember it from…'

'From his brother,' Ross supplied. 'This is how Gavin used to behave.'

The sadness was almost more than she could bear. 'Yes,' she said. 'I see it now. The same technique, too. Gavin used to take phone messages for me, and sometimes they got…scrambled.'

For a moment they both sat in silence. Then she said, 'I'm not in love with his memory any more. Doug has managed to free me of it.'

'What are you going to do about Doug?'

Here at least she was certain. 'Throw him out. I can still feel a bit sorry for him—but he's got to go.'

Ross looked worried. 'I'll come with you. You don't know how he'll react.'

'Seeing you will only make things worse,' she said positively. 'Don't worry about me, I've known Doug for a long time. There'll be no trouble. I'm angry now, and I'm going straight back to tell him.'

'I still think I ought to come with you.' Seeing her determination to cope alone, he went on, 'Well, I'll drive you back and wait outside your flat. You can ring me on my mobile to say that all is well. If you don't phone in fifteen minutes, I'm going to be in there.'

'All right,' she said, rather pleased by his concern. 'I want to do it now, so I think I'll go. Ross, what about us?'

'I told you. We have to trust each other. If we love each other, anything is possible. And we'll sort things out. Can we meet here at lunch-time tomorrow?'

'Nothing will keep me away. Come on, drive me home. There are things I have to do.'

'You're back early,' Doug said. 'They didn't keep you too long on the ward?' He looked relaxed, at ease with his book.

'I didn't go to the ward. I had a drink with Ross McKinnon. We got things sorted out. Doug, I don't know what your stupid game was, but it's over. You lied to me and you lied to my friend. I don't want you here. Now pack your bag and get out!'

Now she had his attention. 'Lyn, you don't mean that! All right, perhaps I did change the messages a bit, but that was only because I care for you. You were looking tired, that man's no good for you. We've got each other, we don't need him. You know what we mean to each other!'

'I know what you mean to me. You mean misery and

grief and memories I wish I didn't have. You've been here long enough. Now get out!'

'But I've got nobody! All I have is you!'

'You don't have me, you never did have! I was engaged to your brother, and now he's dead. Are you going to get out or do I have to call the police?'

She wasn't expecting what happened next. He burst into tears. 'All I've got is you, Lyn, please don't throw me out! Let me stay just a little while longer, just till I get somewhere to go. I'm sorry for what I did, I won't do it again. Please, Lyn!' He stretched out a hand to her. She didn't take it.

The sight of his misery caused some of her anger to evaporate, but not all. Perhaps she could afford to be merciful. 'You can stay till the end of the weekend,' she said. 'Sunday night at the latest, but not a minute longer.' Then something struck her. 'Doug, why didn't you come back to England sooner? What did you do in Borneo?'

He gazed at her with his tear-streaked face. 'I just hung around. Why?'

'You must have spent some time in hospital when you injured your head.'

'Yes. I was in quite some time.'

'What sort of a ward were you in?'

He stood, shoulders stooping. 'I'll go to bed now, Lyn. I'm sorry for what I did.'

'Not yet! Tomorrow you're to see a doctor. I'll give you the address of a good local GP. Sign on with him and ask for a complete check-up. You do it or you're out now.'

'All right, I promise. Goodnight, Lyn.'

She watched him shamble out of the room, then lifted the phone and dialled. 'Ross?'

'Right outside. How did it go, Lyn? Are you all right?'

'No problems at all. He burst into tears. There'll be no more trouble. I told him he could stay till the end of the weekend, to give him a chance to find somewhere to stay.'

Ross wasn't convinced. 'People like him can be cleverer than you think. Be careful, Lyn.'

'I'll be careful. Incidentally, I think I know what's wrong. I suspect he had psychiatric treatment when he was abroad. I've got him to see a doctor tomorrow.'

'Like I said, be careful. Look, I want to come and stay with you for the next couple of days. The sooner that lunatic is out of your life, the better I'll like it.'

Just for a moment she was tempted. Living with Ross would... But, 'He's not really a lunatic,' she said. 'It would be lovely to have you here, but we'll wait until he's gone. Don't forget we've got a date tomorrow lunchtime.'

She felt that he was still anxious. 'Come and stand in the window so I can see you,' he asked.

She opened the curtain, and saw the Land Rover below. She waved and saw a pale shadow wave back. 'I love you,' his voice whispered in her ear.

'We're getting to be regulars,' he said as she walked over to meet him the next day. 'I think I know your tastes so I've ordered for you.' He indicated a ham roll and a lemonade and lime.

'You're a darling. It's been a hard morning on the ward, I need nourishment.' She bit into the roll.

'I like a good trencherwoman. Now, how did last night go? I'm still not sure that it's a good idea for him to be there. You're too soft-hearted, Lyn.'

'He's part of my past and it's good for me to get rid of my own ghosts. It was good of you to offer to help,

Ross, but this I needed to do on my own. Anyway, he's going at the end of the weekend.'

'You sure? You don't think he might try to wear you down? I'm not entirely convinced that you know what you're dealing with.'

'Doug will be no trouble. If he doesn't like it—then too bad. I'm hoping that when he's seen the doctor he might feel better about things. I think he might have had a rough time out there, and he needs therapy.'

'Yes, when he's seen the doctor,' Ross muttered. 'Look, Lyn, one last thing. I want to be there when he goes. Don't tell him I'm coming, I'll just turn up. If he doesn't like it—too bad.'

She thought a moment, then said, 'All right. In fact it might be quite a good idea.'

He didn't seem entirely satisfied with the way she'd agreed to his plan. She noticed the frown on his face, and he looked up at her as if seeking the answer to a question in her eyes. 'Lyn, how soon have you to be back?'

She shrugged. 'You've worked the ward, you know how busy we are. I can only stay a few minutes, and often I don't leave the ward at all. Why? Is there anything wrong?'

He frowned a minute longer, then from his inside pocket took a thick envelope. He laid it on the table between them, and she saw the American stamp. 'Lyn, one thing this affair with Doug proves is that we've got to be open with each other. So I want you to know about this. It's an invitation from AndesAid. They want me to commission and run this hospital in Peru. It's a contract for two years, and I'd start next September.'

'It's the job you've wanted, isn't it?' she asked calmly. 'The excitement of a new place, the chance of climbing on some untouched rock. Are you going to accept?'

'They don't want me till next September. I have plenty of time to make up my mind—they don't want an answer for two or three months.'

'But you very much want to accept, don't you?' She was surprised at her own appearance of calmness, but inside she was in torment.

'It's the kind of job I've always wanted. Up to a few weeks ago I would have accepted like a shot. But now my life is different. You've come into it, and I want you to know about this so that we can decide together.'

'Ross, that's a lot to ask of me! The thought of you not being here... I mean, you know what you mean to me...but I couldn't ask you to stay in England when you so desperately wanted to go to Peru! Every time you thought of it, you'd look at me and think I'd stopped you going. And every time you looked thoughtful, I'd be wondering if you were regretting your decision, and resenting me for keeping you at home.'

'Yes,' he said heavily, 'it is a lot to ask of you, but there is an alternative. You could come with me.'

She had been afraid of this. She didn't want to say anything, but he was entitled to an honest answer. 'You know how I feel about that,' she said. 'I'm a town girl now. I've had my share of wandering round the world. I want to stay put.'

'A house in the suburbs and two-point-four children,' he remembered.

'I've always been honest about it with you,' she said. 'When we first met, you know I tried to avoid you. But you chased me.' After a pause she added, 'And I'm glad you did.'

'So what do we decide?'

'We don't have to decide anything, because, as you

said, there's plenty of time. And let's face it, we still don't
know each other very well. We just wait and see.'

'I feel as if I've known you for ever,' he told her. 'I
don't need time and I don't think you do.'

She had to be hard. 'Ross, there's my career to think
of. I want to press ahead with paediatric neurology and I
can only do that here. And in general...well, I told you.
One Gavin was enough for me. I'm not going through
that again. I won't be left.'

She could guess by the bleakness of his face what he
was thinking. Slowly, he said, 'Well, you've never hidden
that. You've always been honest with me.'

It was hard to see him unhappy. But then, she was
unhappy herself. She said, 'There's absolutely no need for
decisions yet. We still need to spend a lot of time getting
to know each other. Who knows what the future might
bring?' She could see him relaxing slightly. 'Look, how
about a quick meal and a drink at a wine bar tonight? My
treat. There's quite a pleasant one near where I live.'

He smiled. 'I'd like that. Shall I pick you up at half-
past eight?'

She walked back to the hospital on her own, for Ross had
to go back to Everton Heights. Automatically she dodged
heavy-laden shoppers, and waited for pedestrian green
lights, while keeping a wary eye open for traffic. She had
a lot of thinking to do.

What she wanted to do most was to forget about the
job offered to Ross, to concentrate on enjoying the present. They *did* need to get to know each other. She had
made one mistake before, and perhaps she was hurrying
into making another. But even as she thought it, she knew
this wasn't true. Ross was a different kind of man from
Gavin. More than that, they had a different kind of rela-

tionship. She now knew that she had been overtired, emotionally vulnerable, and easily dazzled by Gavin. Ross was different. He gave her space.

But Ross still had the same wanderlust as Gavin. He desperately wanted this job in Peru, and while he was there, she had no doubt that he would want to climb again. She could understand—just—the attraction of being the first to do a climb. To 'put up' a new route. It would be reported in the journals. Who knew, he might call it after her. There would be a kind of immortality.

But there was always the risk. Perhaps this was what drew men to climbing—the knowledge that, if not skilful, or lucky, enough, they might die. They never seemed to think of those they left behind them.

Could she put up with that feeling of pointless loss again? Could she put up with the fear when he was away? She had sworn she'd have nothing to do with a man who would put her through such feelings again, and yet here she was considering it.

Even as she tried to make herself angry at her own foolishness, she knew it was no good. There was one fact, one certainty, that outshone all others. She loved Ross. She couldn't imagine life without him. If he had to go to Peru, then she would accompany him. Better something than nothing at all. But she wouldn't tell him. Not just yet. Who knew what might happen in the next few months?

CHAPTER NINE

BACK on the ward an anxious Merry and an apparently equally anxious Melissa were waiting for her. 'There's a message for you,' Merry said. 'The hospital manager wants you to get in touch with him. He's sent down for the file on Fatima bin Hameed. He says he could access it on the computer, but he likes to read actual notes when he can.'

Lyn had only met Martyn Lennard, the hospital manager, once previously, and had quite taken to him. He had seemed efficient, but pleasant. She had seen him in the distance at the Halloween party and had noted that he'd been one of those who wore fancy dress. In the hospital he was well regarded, being seen as a man who had a difficult job, reconciling the opposing demands of medical excellence and saving money. But what would he want with a humble SHO?

It was unlike Merry to appear so concerned. But personal summonses from the hospital manager were rare. Lyn and Melissa looked at each other thoughtfully, all previous coolness now forgotten. 'I thought we did rather a good job on Fatima,' Melissa said, 'and you certainly spent a lot of time with her.'

'Probably nothing,' Lyn said hopefully. 'Anyway, let's see if we can find out.' She phoned the manager's secretary who asked if they could come up at three for a meeting. Lyn relayed the message to Melissa, who shrugged and nodded. 'Any idea why he wants to see us?' Lyn cautiously asked the secretary.

The secretary, of course, was discreet, but managed to be helpful. 'Well, I think it's not bad news,' she said.

Not bad news. They would have to be happy with that for the next hour.

A smiling secretary showed them straight into the manager's room. Two men stood to greet them. Martyn Lennard was in his customary well-cut grey suit and formal shirt. His guest was in Arab robes. This was not too unusual, for Lizzie's dealt with a lot of children from abroad, and there were many parents who visited in their native dress.

'May I present Sheikh Ali bin Hameed?' said Martyn formally. 'He is the father of Fatima.' The man bowed. Martyn went on, 'The sheikh was unfortunately unable to be with his daughter when she was admitted. His brother brought her.' The sheikh said nothing.

Lyn looked at him closely. He was entirely unlike his portly brother, being a much more imposing man. He was tall, spare of figure, with a lean dark face. Perhaps there was something of Fatima about his eyes, the bones of his cheek and forehead.

Martyn went on, 'Before we get down to business, perhaps you'd like coffee. We have it ready.'

The four sat round a table; there was a brass pot and four small cups, quite unlike the usual hospital mugs. Martyn poured and they drank. The coffee was thick, dark, sweet and stronger than Lyn had ever tasted it before. She wouldn't want it every day, but as an experience it was quite unusual. Obviously it was to suit the sheikh's taste.

It seemed to be understood that they would drink in silence. When they had finished Martyn said, 'The sheikh particularly requested this meeting, and I was very pleased to agree. Sir?'

The man's voice matched his appearance, being deep and powerful. He said, 'I wish to thank you both for what you did for my daughter. Miss Yates, I understand you were responsible for directing my daughter's treatment. Miss Webster, you showed her kindness and care far more than your job dictated. First, I have gifts for you both.'

From the table in front of him he took two packages, and offered them.

Lyn hesitated, then looked at Martyn who nodded imperceptibly. The sheikh had noticed the little exchange and said with a smile, 'I have never been able to understand the Western dislike of accepting gifts. We believe that to give a gift is to honour someone, to accept a gift is to receive an honour. However, I did ask Mr Lennard if offering something would be acceptable. He assured me that in this case there would be no problem.'

'Well, th-thank you,' Lyn stammered. 'Of course we accept. But Fatima is a lovely child, we enjoyed helping her.'

'She is most grateful. I would have been with her, but apparently the world must have oil and so I had meetings in America. My meetings were, I suppose, successful, and I shall reap the benefit over the next ten years. So much so that I wish to give thanks by helping those less fortunate. Your department of neurology where my daughter was treated will also receive money over the next ten years. It is to be spent as your consultant—I think a Mr Henry Birkinshaw—sees fit. Perhaps he will help those from other races, but the decision will be his. I do not mean those of my own race. They are catered for more than adequately.'

Lyn blinked. All this because she had helped a little girl who was lost and frightened?

The sheikh went on. 'Miss Webster, a new hospital is about to be completed in my country. It will have the finest equipment—' he allowed himself a small sardonic smile '—that money can buy. However, equipment is as nothing without skills. I wish to offer you a job in my new hospital. The salary will be...generous.'

She just couldn't cope with all this. There was too much to think about, and it was all becoming unreal. However, she knew she didn't want to leave Lizzie's. She stammered, 'It is very good of you to think of me...but I'm still training. I need to stay here for some years yet to finish my paediatric rotation before I am...before I am fully competent.'

Suddenly a thought struck her. 'But if you are looking for senior staff may I suggest Miss Yates?'

The sheikh nodded. He paused, then added, 'Miss Yates, could my secretary call on you? Perhaps for two or three years you might like to work with us. Once again, the salary will be generous.'

'I'm more interested in the finest equipment you mentioned,' Melissa said, and then, after a hesitation, she said, 'Yes, I am very interested.'

'Excellent! This has been a good day's work.'

Martyn was a skilful manager of people. He realised that this was the right time for his staff to leave. There was more that he needed to discuss with the sheikh in private. He stood. 'Well, we don't want to detain you too long. I know what you're like when you're pulled out of your wards. Dr Yates, Dr Webster, this has been one of the more pleasant of a hospital manager's tasks. I'll be in touch with you and Mr Birkinshaw later.'

There were more goodbyes and thanks and then the two

found themselves outside the office. Perhaps it was reaction, but, giggling, they both flew down the corridor like two schoolchildren.

'Let's open our presents now,' Melissa said when they were far enough from the office. 'I can't go and work until I know what we've got.'

'I feel the same. It's like getting Christmas early.'

There was a deserted waiting area outside a ward, so they sat on two of the chairs. Lyn noted the wrapping paper first—dark grey with an intricate silver pattern. Expensive paper. Inside was a small leather box, with Arabic lettering on the top. She opened the box. There, cushioned by grey velvet, was a bracelet, made of intermeshing strands of three different types, three different colours of gold. It was beautiful! She looked, to see that Melissa had received the same and was sliding it on her wrist. 'It's gorgeous!' she said.

'Are you going to take the job?' Lyn asked.

Melissa stroked the bracelet and said absently, 'You know, I think I will, if it's as good as it sounds. I know I'm too young for a consultancy yet, and I could write two or three papers out there that might help me. Would you come out and stay with me for a couple of months, Lyn?'

Lyn forgot her previous vows never to go to anywhere exotic again. 'You know, I just might,' she said.

It had been an up-and-down day. The elation of receiving the present and the thanks of the sheikh had temporarily made her forget the earlier bad news. But when she got home it returned to haunt her. Ross desperately wanted to take this job, and she didn't want him to go. Ultimately she could think of no way of squaring the circle. The two points of view were irreconcilable. But she was looking forward to taking him for a meal this evening.

She washed her hair, and came into the living room with it swathed in a towel. It was a surprisingly warm evening, so she pushed up the sash window and leaned out for fresh air. The lights of London spread out in front of her, and as ever the view both calmed and exhilarated her. Below, hidden behind the dustbins, she could see the silver gleam of the window cleaner's ladder. She must remember to leave some money out for him.

'Why are you getting dressed up?' Doug asked.

He had been sitting, reading in the living room when she'd come in, responding quietly to her greeting. Now his tone was different, more demanding, and she wasn't going to put up with it.

'It's none of your business but I'm going out with Ross. He's picking me up here later.'

Doug looked uncomfortable, fidgeted a bit, then he said, 'I've got something planned, can't you put him off? I'd like you to go out with me.'

Shortly, she said, 'If you wanted to go out with me you should have asked me in advance. I've already made plans for this evening.'

'Please, Lyn. I know what a trouble I've been to you, but I'm trying to be better now. Can't you put him off just for once?'

He looked up at her, smiling. Again she saw all the charm and guile of her fiancé. She also saw how spurious it was. 'No, I can't put him off. I don't want to. Anyway, where were you planning to take me?'

'I found a jeweller's and arranged for it to stay open. I thought we could pick the ring.'

For a moment she just didn't understand. 'What sort of a ring? I don't know what you're talking about.'

'An engagement ring, of course,' he said impatiently. 'People who get engaged buy a ring. You know that.'

The idea was so appalling it was comic at first. But then she became angry. Had nothing she'd said, nothing they'd agreed, got through to him? 'We're not getting engaged! Whatever gave you that idea? If you were the last man on earth I wouldn't marry you! We were friends once, but now that's finished. After you move out of this flat tomorrow night I never intend to see you again!'

It was harsh but it was how she felt. Then she looked at his suddenly whitened face, and felt the first touch of guilt—and also of apprehension. 'I didn't exactly mean that last bit,' she ventured. 'After you've gone we might meet occasionally and—'

He leaped from his chair and, with a great round-arm swing, slapped her on the side of the face. She was thrown backwards, stumbled over a stool and fell sprawling on the floor. It wasn't so much the pain of the attack, but the shock that appalled her. She wasn't used to violence. It was much more common in hospitals now than it used to be, but so far she had met little of it.

'What…what are you…?'

'You'll not marry anybody but me! First thing you can do is phone that man and tell him not to come round here this evening. I'll be listening, and if you try anything funny you'll suffer because of it!'

The initial pain and shock were now wearing away, to be replaced by a deeper fear. Ross had been right. There was something seriously wrong with Doug. This behaviour was more than erratic, it was dangerously pathological. Doug didn't know what he was doing. If she wasn't careful she might get seriously hurt.

Doug was now crouching in front of her, the telephone

pushed towards her. 'Phone him! Put him off for good, I'll be listening.'

With shaking hands she took the phone and tried to think. This was an emergency. Looking at Doug, now so close to her, she had no doubt that he meant every word he said.

She dialled. Ross answered remarkably quickly, when she had half hoped that he would be out. That would have given her more time to think. Quick, this was an emergency! What could she say?

'I don't want him ringing back!' Doug snapped.

Her voice sounded strained even to herself, somehow she made it sharper. 'Ross,' she said shortly, 'this is Lyn. Now listen, listen very carefully. I don't expect to see you tonight. I've been talking to Doug, he's beside me now. The way things are at present I'll never be going out with you again. Do you understand, Ross? Do you understand?'

There was a pause, and then, 'Yes, I understand perfectly. I think I do. Goodbye.'

He rang off. She hoped he had got the message. She thought he had but...what would he do?

'We'll go to the jeweller's now,' Doug said. 'Sorry I had to hit you, but sometimes these things are necessary, you know.' He smiled at her, that charming, little-boy smile that she now found so sinister.

She indicated the dressing gown she was wearing. 'I can't go out like this. I'm not dressed, I need to—'

'You're all right as you are! You just want to get away from me! Trying to trick me again. I'm not taking you out of the house anyway, I've changed my mind.'

'All right, Doug. We'll sit here and have a quiet evening.'

'I don't like it here now. But we'll make it more like

a home. Come on, I want to get my pictures and books out.'

She had to do as he asked, and he never let her get far from him. They carried books, pictures, the spike of slate and even the detested monkey back to the living room. But he couldn't be bothered to put up the pictures, and stack the books. They remained in great untidy heaps on her floor.

As a doctor she realised that his mood swings were getting more rapid. She would have to be more careful. The thing to do was agree with everything he said and hope...and *hope* that Ross had read her message right. But what would Ross do?

She stood, closed the curtains, then walked to a seat. Doug watched her, carefully noting every movement. When she apparently relaxed in her chair he too relaxed. Now he was mumbling to himself. What on earth was wrong with him? Desperately, to stop herself screaming, she tried to force herself to be a doctor assessing his symptoms. Forget she was alone with him. Imagine they were in hospital, she was taking a history. Whatever it was, it was progressive. She doubted it was psychological in origin. She felt that this was a physiological state.

And it was getting worse. She thought he was getting dangerously unstable. It was no good sitting calmly, agreeing with everything he said, doing whatever he wanted. He was quite likely to take offence at some imaginary slight and attack her again. She didn't want to be hit again, but he was much stronger than she. If she was to fight back she'd only have one chance. Surreptitiously she looked round. There was nothing she could use as a weapon. Yes, there was! There was the spike of slate, that would make a really vicious cosh. She shuddered. Why should she have to think this way? She was a doctor, not a criminal.

Was there anything she could throw through the window? She remembered a lecture she had once attended, on self-defence. The lecturer had told them that a really loud scream was quite a deterrent. It didn't seem much.

There was a slight scraping sound, from somewhere near the window. She looked and saw the curtain billow. Then she remembered, she had left the window slightly open. She needed to distract Doug!

Speaking loudly, she said, 'Just how long are you planning on keeping me here, Doug? We can't stay here for ever, you know. People will wonder where I am.'

It had the desired effect. He paid no attention to his surroundings, but concentrated solely on her. 'I know what I'm doing,' he said angrily. 'None of this would have happened if you'd been reasonable. Carrying on with that Ross fellow when you know you had to marry me.'

'Nothing I ever said or did gave you the right to think that! I just felt sorry for you. You need medical aid, Doug, there's something wrong with you!'

'I am not mad! Don't say that or I'll hit you again, really hard this time!'

He was out of his chair now, moving towards her. Then there was a sudden thump as the sash window was pushed up. The curtains parted, and Ross climbed in between them. 'Done your windows, miss,' he said. 'That'll be eight pounds, please.' She realised he'd used the window cleaner's ladder to get up to her window. It was just the kind of bright idea he would come up with. It must have been the release of tension, but she felt safe now. She laughed, and it was the wrong thing to do.

Doug thought she was laughing at him. 'You tricked

me,' he screamed. 'I'll get you for that!' But he didn't leap at her, he made for Ross.

Ross must have been expecting something of the kind. From his pocket he pulled a canister. But as he moved forward he tripped over one of the piles of books Doug had left on the floor. He fell, and the canister rolled out of his hand under the table. Doug grabbed the spike of slate and raised it over his head, and Lyn knew that it was heavy enough to brain Ross. Desperately she lunged forward and hacked at Doug's shin with her slipper-clad foot. Doug wasn't expecting the sudden attack. He too slipped sideways, crashing over another pile of books. By now Ross had retrieved the canister. He knelt up, aimed it at Doug's face and pressed. There was a hiss, then the smell of the spray. Doug screamed, clutched his face with both hands, and collapsed, choking and sobbing.

For a moment Ross watched him warily, then climbed to his feet and came over to Lyn. He put his arms round her, pulled her close. 'Are you all right? Has he hurt you at all?'

She pressed her head into his chest. 'No. He slapped me once, but it was nothing much. Oh, Ross, he went mad! I thought he was going to kill me!'

'It's all right, it's all right,' he soothed. 'I'm here now and it's all right.'

She wanted so much to stay here, so close to him. He was warm and he was solid, there was the movement of his chest against hers and the reassuring smell of him, half cologne, half male warmth. But she was still a doctor.

'What did you do to Doug?' she asked. 'What did you spray him with?'

'It's a form of CS gas. It's nasty stuff but it's not long-term dangerous. I called in at the hospital and borrowed it from Jock MacGregor, Head of Security. Incidentally,

I must phone him. He said that if I didn't, in half an hour he'd ring the police.'

Reality was creeping in now, there were decisions to make, and things they had to do. The first decision was what to do with Doug. 'Do we have to involve the police?' she asked.

'How d'you feel? Are you sure he hasn't hurt you? Or harmed anyone else?'

'I'm certain.'

'Then we'll see if we can deal with it ourselves. First I've got to phone Jock and thank him, then I'll see if I can call in a favour. Doug should be all right, but d'you want to irrigate his eyes? It might help.'

Ross seemed to have taken complete control, for which she was glad. She fetched a bowl, filled it with water and bathed Doug's eyes. He allowed her to help him to his feet, and sit him in a chair. All the fight seemed to have gone out of him, and he was as pliable as a doll. But she noticed that Ross kept an eye on him.

Ross made two quick calls then nodded at her. 'We're in luck. Malcolm Saville is a pal of mine, a neurosurgeon at a sister hospital to Everton Heights. He'll admit Doug at once, and see what can be done for him. It's likely that Doug's condition is physical in origin. If so Malcolm will deal with it. But if it's psychological then we'll have to send him somewhere else. Malcolm says that if there's any paperwork, and details of treatment that Doug might have had abroad, then he'd like to see it. I take it that Doug hasn't seen a doctor in this country?'

'No,' she said. 'He's just back from Borneo. If you keep an eye on him I'll see what I can find.'

She didn't like rummaging through Doug's things, but she knew it was necessary. In the end she found what she was looking for, stuffed in an inside pocket of the great

rucksack he had brought in with him. A crumpled letter
from an Australian doctor who had treated Doug in
Borneo. It was intended for the doctor—any doctor—
Doug should have seen the day he arrived home. It de-
scribed the injuries Doug had sustained in his fall, the
treatment given, and then the doctor's growing belief that
there was something else wrong. The doctor had had neither the knowledge nor the equipment to deal with it.

'There's a letter from a doctor in Borneo,' she said,
passing it to Ross. 'It looks like he was the only doctor,
working in one of these little bush hospitals. He did the
best he could for Doug, but he knew it wasn't enough.'

Ross scanned the letter, nodded. 'You're right. Let's
get this man somewhere where he might be cured.'

'I'm going to write to that Australian doctor,' Lyn said.
'I'm impressed by what he's done. What he's worked out
largely by guesswork.'

'I'm sure he'll appreciate it.' Ross grinned and winked
at her. 'Send him a photograph of yourself and he'll think
it all worthwhile.'

'Come on, you! Be serious! Oh!' She looked down.
'I'm still in my dressing gown. Give me a minute, I'll
dress.'

'I was wondering if you'd notice. Go on, get dressed,
Doug and I will be all right.'

Doug's quietness was causing her to worry. What could
be wrong with him? They needed expert advice.

When she was dressed they each took one of Doug's
arms and half carried him downstairs. He allowed himself
to be guided, and strapped into the front seat of the Land
Rover, without the slightest objection.

Ross's friend Malcolm Saville was a surprise. About
Ross's age, he was a short square man with vast shoulders
and hair cut so short that it appeared as little more than a

shadow. 'This thug is quite a competent neurosurgeon,' Ross told her. 'But don't say I said so or he might get vain and think of growing his hair.'

'Pleased to meet you, Lyn,' Malcolm said courteously to her. 'If you ever think of forming more than a distant friendship with this man, please consult me first. I can tell you stories of his behaviour that will curl your hair. Struck off? He should never have been struck on. I wouldn't enlist him in the St John Ambulance Brigade.'

She giggled. She liked him at once.

They made their way to a side ward. Doug was now completely quiescent, saying nothing and following where he was led. Lyn noticed Malcolm watching him, and suspected that those shrewd brown eyes were missing little.

'I'll examine my patient now,' Malcolm said, 'then I'll get a nurse to give him a sedative and put him to bed. You two can drink coffee in my room till I've finished and then I'll take a history from you, Lyn. Were there any medical details that you could find?'

Ross handed him the letter. 'Ah,' said Malcolm after a quick scan, 'now this is interesting.'

In Malcolm's room there were so many of the textbooks that Lyn recognised. She wandered round, picking them up, opening them, glancing and then replacing them. She couldn't settle. Ross recognised and respected her mood.

'Too much has happened,' he told her. 'You're hyper, not sure what to do next. You can't rest.'

'I don't need a doctor to tell me that,' she snapped back, and then caught him smiling at her. 'I don't know what you're laughing at, anyone would think...' For a moment she heard herself and then had to laugh. 'All right, I know the state I'm in. It's just that—'

'To a certain extent you're in a state of shock,' he told

her. 'In a few minutes it'll hit you. You'll be so tired you'll fall asleep in that chair. But not yet. You need to talk to Malcolm first. Now, have some coffee.'

Fortunately it wasn't long before Malcolm returned. 'An interesting case, an interesting man,' he said, 'and before you ask I'm not going to say a thing until I've done more tests. First thing in the morning we'll give him an MRI scan. I suspect that will tell us plenty.'

Lyn nodded. A magnetic resonance imaging scan could show if there was any damage inside the skull, or anything pressing on the brain.

'There is one point,' Malcolm went on. 'Who's the next of kin?' He looked at Lyn.

'He never knew his father and his mother abandoned him when he was four,' she said flatly. 'His only brother is dead and as far as he knows he has no relations at all in the world.'

'I see. I find that entirely believable.' He took a large pad from a drawer and unscrewed his fountain pen. 'Now, Lyn, I want you to tell me all about his behaviour when you first knew him, and then exactly how he has behaved over the past few days. Ross, would you——?'

'Please, I want Ross to stay,' she interrupted. 'I'm feeling a little...unsteady.'

'All right,' Malcolm said after a pause. 'But, Ross, you keep quiet. Now, when exactly did you first meet...?'

Taking the history was a long process. Some of it was painful, for Malcolm needed to know something of her relationship with Doug when she was still engaged to his brother. And then, when he questioned her about the time since Doug had arrived on her doorstep, she felt a great anger at herself. What had happened was so obvious! She was hoping to be a neurosurgeon herself—why hadn't she spotted the signs of illness? She said this to Malcolm and he sighed.

'Seeing the obvious is very difficult when you're close to the subject,' he said. 'That's why you should never try to be doctor to your own family. Now, that's all I need for now. When I get any news I'll give you a ring. It should be some time tomorrow.'

Ross spoke for the first time for a while. 'We're grateful to you, Malcolm. If ever you need—'

'Don't you worry, I'll ask,' Malcolm said cheerfully. 'Don't forget, Lyn. Keep this man at a distance!'

'I'll try,' she said, 'but do you know he climbed through my living room window tonight?'

She was fine until she was sitting in his Land Rover. Then it hit her. With a little moan she slumped against him. Instantly his arm was round her. 'I know,' he said softly, 'it all seems too much and you can't cope and you didn't want this anyway. We're going straight back to your flat and you're going to bed.'

She managed to peek at her watch. It was only ten o'clock! 'I was taking you out for a meal,' she said unsteadily. 'We were going to that wine bar and—'

'Blood sugar!' he shouted. 'Lyn, what have you had to eat since we met at lunch-time?'

That was easy. 'Nothing,' she said.

'No wonder you're feeling down. We'll have to feed you. Now where...?'

'Please, I don't want to go to a restaurant,' she said. 'I'm not dressed for it, I look a mess and I just don't want to face more people.'

'You don't look a mess to me. But I didn't intend to take you anywhere, I don't even intend to cook for you, though I could. We'll get a take-away.'

'A take-away,' she said wonderingly, as if it were some strange new brilliant idea. 'I never thought of a take-away.'

They were nearly back at the flat when he stopped outside a brilliantly illuminated shop front, garish with red, blue and yellow neon. He was back within two minutes, and on the seat between them he put a warm, good-smelling brown paper parcel. Her stomach growled in anticipation and they both laughed.

When they got back to the flat she didn't want to go back into the living room. He sensed this, led her straight to the kitchen and sat her at the table. Anyone would think he lived here, she mused, as he seemed to find everything they needed: plates, mugs, cutlery, vinegar and sauce without any difficulty. He switched on the kettle.

'The ultimate British comfort food,' he said, opening the brown paper parcel with a flourish. 'Fish, chips and mushy peas.' He opened her bread bin. 'Butter your own bread.'

The smell was entrancing, and she realised that she was famished. 'This looks good,' she muttered, and reached for her fork. It was good too. They ate in silence, drank the tea that he made, and afterwards she felt so much better.

'I needed that and it did me good.' She sighed. 'Now I can rejoin the human race.'

'It was a good meal,' he agreed. 'I suspect that if I was to have my last ever meal it wouldn't be steak or lobster but fish and chips. We'll go there again. Now, I'll clear away while you have a bath. You'll feel even better.'

'Ross! This is my flat, and you've done everything so far. At least let me wash up!'

'Doctor's orders,' he said imperturbably. 'You've had

a stressful time, now you need to relax. I'll see you to bed and then I'll be off.'

'You're not going to stay?'

He heard the slight uncertainty in her voice. 'I certainly am. I've slept on many couches in my time, why should yours be left out? Now off to your bath and leave me to my washing-up liquid.' It seemed simplest to do what he said.

She enjoyed her bath and it did undo more knots in her still upset mind, but she didn't stay in too long. She put on her dressing gown, took a great armful of bedding from her linen cupboard and went to the living room.

'I'm a very good housewife,' he said. 'I've tidied up a bit as well.'

She blinked. He had taken all the piles of books and moved them, presumably, back next door. The ornaments and pictures were gone too. Her living room was as she wanted it: peaceful, calming. She hadn't been looking forward to having to move everything and guessed that he knew this.

'Wonderful,' she said. 'Now this is a bit of a change from the last time we...er...spent some time together. This time you borrow my towels and spare toothbrush. But I haven't a dressing gown that will come anywhere near you, so you'll have to wrap a towel round you.'

He looked at the bundle of bedding she was carrying. 'Don't go to a lot of trouble,' he said. 'I can sleep anywhere, I'm used to the hard ground. Why not go to bed and leave me to...?'

'I'm feeling better!' she snapped. 'Leave me to organise my own home and go and get a bath.'

'Yes, miss,' he said.

The minute he had left the room she started on her carefully thought out arrangements.

He came back into the room twenty-five minutes later. He was dressed solely in a towel round his waist, and she thrilled to see his still wet hair, the powerful muscles of chest and shoulder, the trim waist. 'Lyn?' he queried.

'You said you didn't mind a hard surface,' she said, 'so you can sleep on the carpet. We both will. It's quite thick and so it's quite comfortable.'

She rather enjoyed his expression of bewilderment. She had made a double bed on the floor, with pillows from her own bed and her own duvet. The room was in semi-darkness; she had lit five candles and lined them along the hearth. She had inherited a love of candlelight from her parents.

'There are two glasses and an open bottle of red wine here,' she went on. 'I know it's a wine you will like. So why don't you take off that towel and come to bed? With me.'

She was lying in the bed, but as she spoke she leaned sideways and reached for the bottle. He knew then that she was naked, her arms, shoulders, and breasts showing in the flickering candlelight.

'But you're still upset,' he said hoarsely. 'Perhaps...I thought you should...'

'I shall be upset if you don't come to bed,' she interrupted. 'Please take off that towel.'

He did. For a moment she had a sight of him naked, making clear his need for her. Then he slipped in beside her. He smelled of French Fern, her expensive soap, and it was strange to smell it on someone else. She felt his leg touch hers, the weight of his body pull at the duvet. 'Sit up and drink your wine,' she said. 'I'm going to enjoy mine.' She sat up in bed and handed him a glass.

It was a good wine, she had bought half a dozen bottles a few days previously, wanting to have something special for the next time he should call. She had not expected anything like this, though. He sat up too, and they drank sitting hip to hip as she enjoyed each rich mouthful.

It was both intimate and companionable. There was no way she could sit up in bed and pretend to be modest, so she was not going to try to hold the duvet under her chin. From the waist up he could see her and she revelled in the joy it gave her, and the knowledge of the passion it was rousing in him.

'You're gorgeous,' he whispered. 'I've just a spoonful of wine left...but I don't want to drink it out of my glass.' Carefully he leaned over and poured just a little of the rich red liquid on the slope of each breast. She shivered at the unexpected coolness as the wine ran down to the roughness of her nipples.

'I said I wanted to drink it.' He leaned over her, took her glass from her and pushed her backwards. Then, delicately, he touched each tiny rivulet of wine with his tongue, and she shivered again, but this time with delight at the warmth of him. The shiver turned into a gasp as he took each now burgeoning peak into his mouth, sucking, caressing, even biting her so gently.

Her arms wrapped round his neck. 'Love me,' she murmured. 'Love me.'

Perhaps they were both more tired than they realised. Their love-making was more languorous than before. It was important to get to know each other, to feel each other's body, to know once again that it was more rewarding to give pleasure than to receive it. Their final joint climax was not the peak of ecstasy that it had been before, but rather something that they knew was coming and could meet together. She held him, kissed him, and as their bodies met and shuddered she knew that this was a togetherness far beyond the physical. This man was hers, just as she was his. They must always be together.

CHAPTER TEN

LYN was a doctor, she was used to going without sleep. But next morning she wouldn't have stirred if Ross hadn't tried to slide quietly out of bed.

'Where are you going?' she mumbled sleepily. 'I don't want you to leave me.'

He bent over to kiss her forehead. 'I'm going to work. And as I told you, you're going to take the morning off. There'll be no problem, I'll fill in for you.'

'But I feel fine! I don't need to take...'

He pressed her gently back. 'Doctor's orders. I think you need to take things easy for a few hours more. Come in at lunch-time—by then there should be some news about Doug. Do you want to go and get into your own bed?'

'No. I've been so happy here.' She smiled mischievously. 'Will you come and kiss me again before you go?'

'Nothing will stop me. In fact, I'm tempted to...' She stretched out her arms to him. 'I'm going,' he said with groan, 'but it's hard.' The warm naked body next to hers slipped away.

She was going to do as he said; she was going to stay in bed. She wasn't exactly ill, and happily there was no bruising where Doug had slapped her. But she felt as if she needed a rest from the constant need to make decisions, about her own life as well as about her patients. Decisions were hard, painful, so she would sleep and for a while she could put them off. And she had been so happy in this hastily thrown-together bed.

Dimly she heard him moving about her flat, the hiss of the shower, the clang of the kettle. Then he was back with her again, a mug of tea for her in his hand.

'You smell of my soap again,' she said when he leaned over her. 'It's rather nice.'

'It'll make me think of you through the morning,' he said.

When he tried to kiss her on the forehead again she grabbed him, and for a brief while pulled him onto the warmth of her body. 'Last night was wonderful,' she said. 'Now you'd better go before I wake up properly. Otherwise you'll never be off.'

He kissed her properly then, allowing his hands to roam over her naked shoulders, her back, holding her close to him. Then he stood. 'Not before lunch-time,' he growled.

'I'll do as you say.' And she would. As the door clicked shut behind him she closed her eyes again. For another two or three hours she would sleep, dreaming of the happiness that had been hers, and forgetting the world where there were bleak decisions to make.

In the end she just couldn't do it. She did sleep for far longer than usual, but then she had to get up. She tidied the living room, sadly putting away the sheets that had made their impromptu double bed. Then there were the books and other things that Doug had brought out. She went next door to where Ross had neatly stacked them and made a decision. They would all have to go. She would wait till Doug was recovered, offer him whatever he wanted of them, and throw away the rest. And she would not store them for him. They were going to be out of her life for good.

When the flat was to her liking, she made herself more tea and had a bath. A bath in the morning was a small treat—usually there was only time for a quick shower. And once in the bath she had to face up to what she had been doing. Thinking about Doug had only been a displacement activity. She had made her decision; he was no longer a problem for her. Now she had to consider what to do about Ross. This was the vital decision she had to take. She loved him. Should she tell him she was willing to go to Peru with him?

Perhaps, if you were in love, you should make sacrifices. She knew how he could make her so happy; why should she not seize on that happiness? And then she thought of the misery she had suffered—admittedly, at the hands of someone entirely different. But would she ever be able to sit contentedly at home, knowing that the man she loved was deliberately risking his life?

There was no smart answer to her questions. She sighed, drank her tea and got out of the bath.

'I've had a rest,' she told him as she came onto the ward. 'I feel a lot better but now I think I need to work.'

He looked at her expressionlessly. 'As you wish,' he said. 'I'd like you to clerk Jessica Nicholls, aged five. She's just come in. Jessica is doing fine, she's comforting her mother who is a nervous wreck.'

'Fine.' This wasn't an uncommon situation. 'I'll get on with it at once. Er, when will you...?'

'I've had a phone call from Malcolm. He'll have the results of most of the tests by one o'clock, and he promised to phone me again then. Meet me for lunch at quarter past?'

'I'd like that,' she said, 'but not at the pub. Can we simply go down to the canteen?'

'Certainly. But it'll make people talk. You won't be able to hold my hand under the table.'

'I will if I want to,' she said stoutly. 'I'll see you down there. I'll get you a salad or something.'

'Don't you think that I'm entitled to something a bit more substantial?' he asked, and smiled when she blushed.

'I'll go and do my clerking,' she said.

She could tell that the news was good—well, at least, not bad—as he walked towards her in the canteen.

'Malcolm told me to take notes,' he said as he sat opposite her, pulling out a notebook. 'He said word of mouth wasn't accurate enough.'

'Never mind the full diagnosis,' she said impatiently, 'just tell me—is he going to be all right?'

'Is it important to you?'

With a tiny touch of pleasure she wondered if he was just slightly jealous. But... 'It's very important to me,' she said. 'If he's seriously ill then I suppose I have some responsibilities towards him. He's got no one else. But I want him well so he can get out of my life for ever.'

'That's a bit hard,' he suggested.

'Sometimes you need to be hard. Otherwise people take advantage of you. Never again! I intend...' Suddenly she heard what she was saying, and realised what conclusions he might draw. 'Ross, you know I was talking about Doug and...and Gavin, don't you? I wasn't talking about you.'

He smiled, reached over and rubbed her forearm. 'I know that. And I think that you're still a little shocked by the events of last night. But back to Doug. Yes, Malcolm thinks he is probably going to be all right. Doug's had an MRI scan and also a blood test. The blood test was interesting, because it showed a very high concentration of leucocytes.'

'Leucocytes? They're the body's way of fighting infec-

tion. That suggests there is some inflammation somewhere. But where...?'

'Think,' he suggested. 'No sign of any kind of abscess
on the body. So?'

'Something internal.' She knew that abscesses could
form almost anywhere in the body. 'And with the strange
behaviour it would probably be the brain.'

'Quite right. Doug has a tropical cerebral abscess. On
the right frontal lobe of the brain. That Australian doctor
was right in his suspicions, but he thought Doug's behaviour change might have been brought on by the lesions
caused when he fell off that rock face. He just didn't have
the facilities to do all the tests he wanted to.'

'So what will Malcolm do?'

'First he'll drill through the skull and put a drain in, to
get rid of the pus. He'll put Doug on a course of antibiotics to get rid of the infection, which might even be
caused by tuberculosis. With any luck Doug will recover
when the pressure is removed. If he doesn't, then Malcolm
will operate and cut out the abscess. But he thinks that
when he's finished that everything will be all right, Doug
will be back to normal.'

. 'That's wonderful,' she said. Just for once she was seeing medicine from the outside, and she felt so grateful for
what it could do.

Ross was still interested in Doug. 'What d'you think
he'll do when he's discharged?' he asked.

'Doug will be off,' she said. 'I don't know where but
somewhere. He'll be embarrassed about how he treated
me and he won't want to see me again. I decided this
morning to tell him that he can take any of Gavin's things,
and those he doesn't want I'm going to throw out.'

'Is that a symbolic action?'

'No,' she said with certainty, 'it's a practical one. I need the room. Now, there's something else we have to discuss.'

He looked at her in mock alarm. 'When you become businesslike you do it properly,' he said. 'This super-efficient Lyn is a new creature.'

'No, it's not. I'm always like this. Now concentrate! Last night you were supposed to be my guest, and I was to take you to dinner at the local wine bar. I was going to dress up a bit, we were going to have a good bottle of wine, with a pleasant meal and a chat. In general we were going to have a civilised and enjoyable evening. Instead of which we had a fight, a trip to the hospital and fish and chips.'

'I enjoyed the fish and chips. And what came afterwards.'

'Don't try to make me blush, it won't work. Well, only a bit. Now, I felt cheated out of my evening yesterday. So may I take you to dinner this evening?'

'I'll be at your flat at eight.'

Perhaps it was the contrast with the troubles of the night before. But for some reason everything seemed perfect with their evening. She wore the red dress she had put out ready. In it she felt both smart and attractive, and she noted the glances from women as well as men as she walked into the wine bar.

Ross had arrived carrying a bunch of lilies, and she loved the long stalks, the fragile blooms. They had walked down, to be given a secluded corner banquette. The food and drink had been superlative, and the thick Rioja had been the right wine to drink with their tender steaks. The service had been unobtrusive but effective.

'Altogether, a wonderful meal,' Ross said as the waiter put a pot of coffee before them.

'Not finished yet,' she countered. 'We'll have something with this. Brandy, or something a bit sweet?'

They settled for Glayva, the Scotch liqueur.

'You've got an expression on your face that's making me wary,' he said as he settled himself comfortably in the banquette. 'You look as if you're going to make a speech, but you're not quite sure how to start. I hope it's going to be something nice.'

She was shocked that she was so transparent. But then, this man now knew her better than anyone she'd ever met. He could feel her moods, react to them. They were so close!

'I think it's something nice,' she said. 'But it's only half formed, and I'm still not sure what I mean or how to say it.'

He said nothing, but leaned over as he so often did, and stroked her wrist.

'It's about us,' she said, 'and what you told me about the job in Peru. Now, I know there's quite a lot of time before you have to make up your mind, and all kinds of things might happen before then. And I think we need a breathing space. We'll go on working together, seeing each other, but not making decisions.'

'I think that's a good idea,' he agreed. 'What I think we feel for each other—we don't want to rush it.'

'I told you that I wouldn't go with you. Not under any circumstances. Well, I've been thinking, and I've decided that that was giving you an ultimatum. I don't want to threaten you, Ross. We'll wait and see—but I'd be far happier with you in Peru than without you in England. If you want me to go, I will.'

He was about to speak but she overrode him. '*And*,' she said, 'it would be my decision. I would never say you had talked me into anything, or persuaded me to do something I didn't want.'

She sipped her Glayva. 'I want to stay with you always, Ross. I love you.'

It wasn't like Henry. Lyn had phoned him that morning, asking him to come down to the ward to check on one of his cases, Annette Dowling, a little girl whose temperature remained obstinately high. Her condition hadn't been too serious, but Lyn had wanted an expert opinion. Henry had come three hours later, and Lyn and Merry had accompanied him as he'd looked at the little girl, pursed his lips and written out an altered prescription. 'With any luck this should do it,' he said. 'She's been here long enough. Now I think that should do for today.'

'If you have a minute I'd like you to have a look at young Harry Edmonds,' Lyn suggested. 'I'm just a bit worried—'

'I know the case,' Henry interrupted. 'Unless there's been a radical change in condition there's no need to worry, he'll keep till tomorrow morning.'

Lyn was a little surprised at this. Henry was usually only too pleased to discuss a case with her. But he had been offhand with both her and Merry. Polite, of course, but not appearing to pay much attention to what they were saying. Or, indeed, to his patient. Not like the ever-enthusiastic Henry at all.

Perhaps he realised this. As Merry walked away he turned to Lyn and said, 'I feel a little out of sorts today. The hospital manager is a decent chap, but getting extra funding out of him is harder than finding a collapsed vein. I've had a stressful week.'

Henry complaining about stress? she thought. Usually

he thrives on it. But she said, 'I suppose all the other departmental heads are looking for extra money, too?'

'As ever.' Henry stood with his head bent. 'Lyn, I'll just run over these files in the doctors' room. I wonder if I could ask you to fetch me a cup of coffee? I do feel the need of some kind of pick-up.'

Stranger and stranger. Henry had never asked anyone to fetch his coffee, not even the most junior nurse. But she was happy to oblige.

For various reasons the little doctors' room on the ward wasn't much used. Mostly they congregated in Merry's room, which was where the coffee was made. But if Henry wanted his coffee in the doctors' room, he should have it. Lyn made two coffees, and took them along.

'I've brought myself a drink as well,' she said cheerfully as she kneed open the door. 'But if you want to work in quiet...Henry!' Her voice rose to a shriek.

Henry was sitting, slumped forward over the table, his right hand grasping his chest. His face was pale and clammy; she could hear his rapid breathing. And from his tortured expression it was obvious that he was in agony.

But he hadn't lost consciousness and he was still a doctor. 'Heart, Lyn,' he gasped. 'It's my heart.'

Lyn looked back in the corridor, saw a passing junior nurse. 'Get Sister in here *now*,' she snapped. 'This is an emergency.'

Then she turned, took Henry's wrist, and noted the rapid pulse. She was almost certain that Henry was right. He was suffering a coronary thrombosis—a heart attack. It was one of the commonest causes of death in older men. One of the arteries leading to the heart had become blocked, probably by a thrombus, or clot.

The pain would be intense. Even a doctor needed comfort, encouragement, and sympathy at a time like this. Lyn put her arm round Henry, eased him back in his chair and supported his feet. 'It's going to be all right,' she said calmly. 'We'll get help, we'll get something for the pain and you'll be fine.'

Somehow Henry managed to joke. 'Of course I will.'

Merry bustled into the room. 'I think Henry's had a coronary,' Lyn said quietly. 'Can you ring down to the chest section? I know they don't usually deal with adults, but they probably know more about it than we do.'

Merry took the situation calmly—that was what made her such a good sister. And she knew everybody in the hospital. She lifted the telephone. 'Matt Roberts is consultant there, he'll be able… Hello, Sister? Alice? Oh, good. Look, we think we have an emergency coronary…no, not a patient, it's Henry Birkinshaw, our consultant, we're in the doctors' room in Neurology… Who have you got handy? Great…thirty seconds.'

'We're in luck,' she muttered to Lyn. 'Matt Roberts himself is on his way up.'

She looked at Henry with an expert's eye. 'Thank goodness he hasn't arrested. But we could always manage mouth to mouth and cardiac massage if necessary.' It wasn't unusual after a coronary thrombosis for the heart to stop entirely. However, prompt action could keep the patient alive.

The door banged open, and in came the white-coated figure of Matt Roberts. 'Causing trouble again, Henry? Let's have a look at you.' He bent over Henry's resting figure, then turned and looked at Lyn questioningly.

'He was working until five minutes ago,' Lyn said, 'though he did say that he didn't feel too good. I went to fetch him a coffee and when I came back he was like this. I haven't examined him or offered any treatment.'

'Good.' There was a rattle outside the door, and someone tapped. 'That'll be my trolley,' Matt said. 'I've found a full-sized one. I've got a side ward he can go into temporarily—I want him where I can stabilise him.'

The trolley was pushed in by a burly male nurse, and he helped Matt lift Henry onto it. 'Down to my ward and we'll get you some morphine and oxygen,' Matt said gently to Henry. 'You'll feel a lot easier then. Later on we'll sort out some thrombolytic drugs.'

Henry apparently tried to whisper something, and Matt leaned over to listen.

'Don't worry, Henry. The department will be fine without you, the work'll be done. I'll get someone to fetch in one of your SRs.'

He looked questioningly at Lyn. 'I think Ross McKinnon is in his room,' she said, 'but I know both SRs will want to be informed.'

'Leave it to you, then. Come on, Henry. You're going for a ride.'

The door banged open again, and the trolley was carefully manoeuvred out.

'Please,' Lyn called out desperately after them, 'will you let us…?'

'We'll call as soon as there's any news. Don't worry, this is serious but not dangerous yet.' The trolley was hastened down the corridor.

'You've had a shock,' Merry said practically. 'For that matter, so have I. It's always hard for a doctor when it's someone you know. Come on, we'll sit down ourselves for ten minutes. We deserve it.'

'I'll phone Ross first,' Lyn said. Merry was right. She felt sick, and upset.

This was a side of Ross that she had never seen before. He was efficient. First he came to the ward to see if there was anything that needed his attention urgently. Then he phoned the hospital manager and said that they would need additional senior staff for a while, could they arrange a prompt meeting with Matt Roberts? He would contact Melissa and should he fetch Henry's wife? Martyn Lennard came down and visited the ward, then disappeared in search of Ross. Shortly afterwards Melissa phoned the ward, she was on her way into hospital to see Henry, but would Lyn page her if she was needed urgently?

'We can't lose Henry,' she said. 'I...we need him. He's always been there for me. I'm going to phone my dad.'

Lyn was rather surprised. Melissa had always seemed calm, self-contained, and rather cool. But her voice on the phone was decidedly shaky. Melissa was very upset. 'He's going to be all right,' Lyn said. 'Matt Roberts got to him very quickly. He phoned up after half an hour and said Henry was stabilised and more comfortable, that there was no immediate danger.'

'What about long term?' Melissa asked.

Lyn had no answer. Both of them knew how dangerous a heart attack could be to a man of Henry's age.

There was still the general work of the ward to be done, and at the end of the afternoon Ross came in to see her.

She followed him into the doctors' office, and hugged him when they were alone inside. She thought he needed to be hugged as much as she did. Usually his face was calm, amiable, but now it showed obvious lines of stress. 'Been a hard afternoon,' he said.

'Tell me about Henry.'

'Matt Roberts did a super job stabilising him, but this is a paediatric hospital. An ambulance has taken Henry to a hospital for adults, Melissa's father has come in and taken charge of him. So far the prognosis is good. But I wish it hadn't happened.'

'Why Henry?' Lyn asked wearily. 'He doesn't smoke, he doesn't eat or drink too much, he isn't overweight, he plays golf regularly. What more could he do? It doesn't seem fair.'

'It isn't fair. But Henry did two things wrong. Firstly he worked far too hard—he was under pressure. And secondly he had parents who both died of a heart attack. Another fifteen years and we might know which genes are responsible for the condition. But not yet.'

'When can I see him?'

'I suggest tomorrow afternoon some time. His wife's with him now, but he's pretty groggy. I doubt he'll even know it's you.'

Ross stood, then, to her surprise, leaned over and kissed her. 'I'm acting consultant for a while,' he said, 'and there's plenty of work. Perhaps I won't see as much of you as I'd wish. But I want you to know that when I'm not working I'm thinking of you. Often I even think of you when I *am* working.'

'That's lovely to know,' she told him.

She did visit Henry the next day. He recognised her, she knew, but he said little. She sat with him for a while, chatted about work on the ward and then left. As she walked down the corridor she saw the theatre-greens clad figure of Sir Sidney bounding towards her. 'Lyn! Good to see you.'

'Sir Sidney. Good to see you too. You're looking after my boss properly?'

'Of course I am, we medical men have to stick together. Now, look, I'm in a hurry as usual, but there's something you need to know. If you can, bring a bit of pressure to bear. I don't like saying this—but Henry must *not* go back to working as he was. I'm telling his friends and colleagues because I know what Henry's like. Persuade him and keep in touch!' And Sir Sidney was off.

She had guessed this would be the case, but to hear it said so authoritatively by Sir Sidney rather upset her. Henry loved his work, and would hate to lose it.

Four days later Ross rang her. Because of his increased workload they had not had chance to meet again, but he phoned her for a chat every night and she loved it. This was something different.

'Henry wants to see us both tonight,' he said. 'Says it's important. Can you meet me at the hospital about eight?'

'Easily. He is all right?'

Ross chuckled. 'All too much all right. He asked for some hospital files to be brought in so he could check them. Sir Sidney had to forbid it. Now, after we've met Henry can we forget everything we've got to do and go for a meal?'

'Would you like another take-away? More fish and chips in my flat?' She might as well be brazen. 'You could stay the night if you wanted.'

'That I would love. See you at eight, then.'

She replaced the receiver, smiling faintly. That was forward, she thought to herself approvingly.

Henry was much better. He was sitting up in bed, a sweater visible rather than pyjamas, with books stacked on his cabinet. His face was alert but Lyn thought she could detect signs of the ordeal he had been through. There were new lines by his eyes, perhaps a downturn to his mouth, but his voice was as firm as ever.

'It's good to see you both,' he said. 'Sir Sidney has been in to tell me that I must not try to run my department from this hospital bed, but just for once I'm going to defy him.'

He looked round at the little side ward and said quietly, 'I think every doctor should spend some time as a patient. It gives you a new perspective on things.'

Lyn realised then just what a shock he had received.

'However...' Henry's voice was stronger '...Sir Sidney, as usual, has been more than forthright. He tells me that there is damage to the muscles of the heart, that if I try to resume work he guarantees I'll be dead within a year.'

To hear it put so bluntly shocked Lyn. But she knew it was certainly true.

'I have heard it said that men under sentence of death speak truly,' Henry went on. 'I am not under sentence of death, but I have thought about what I am going to say. Ross, I can no longer be Consultant Neurosurgeon to St Elizabeth's. Who is going to take my place? There are not too many senior paediatric neurosurgeons available, and, of them all, you are the best. Ross, if you don't take up this place you will be failing in what you know to be your duty.'

Lyn gulped. She had never heard Henry talk this way before.

Neither, apparently, had Ross. 'Henry, this is emotional blackmail,' he said.

'Blackmail, certainly. But not emotional. You know as well as I do the neurosurgeons who will apply for my job. Can you name me one person who would be as good as you? I expect you to be honest.'

Fascinated, Lyn watched Ross's face. She could almost detect the thoughts that swirled through his mind, the power of Henry's argument, the list of possible candidates considered and then rejected, perhaps some disappointment. Then, 'You know I was thinking of going to Peru for a couple of years,' he said.

'I do. Medically, you will be more use here. If you stay with us we will use money given to the department by Sheikh bin Hameed to offer a scholarship to a Peruvian from the hospital to come and train to be a doctor. Ultimately, a full-time doctor would be more use to them than you would be for just two years.'

'More blackmail!'

'Certainly. In my own way I am a very unscrupulous man.' Henry looked entirely satisfied with himself. 'Now I know this is all most unfair, but I would like you to think about what I have said. Incidentally, Martyn Lennard knows about this and agrees with me.'

Once again Lyn studied Ross's face. She hadn't had time fully to take in all that had been said, but she was desperate to hear what he would say.

For a while he said nothing. Both Lyn and Henry watched him, and Lyn thought Henry slumped a little in the bed. Then, 'You can sleep easy, Henry,' Ross said. 'I'll apply for the position when it comes vacant, and, if I get it, I hope I'll be as successful, and as cunning, as you. I'm thinking of settling down anyway.'

'You could always spend a couple of months in Peru when you've got established,' Henry said. 'Now, I'm feeling a bit tired. Call on me again?'

The London streets were crowded as they walked out of the hospital gates. 'I think you need a drink,' Lyn said. 'You've had something of a shock.'

'I agree. That looks a quiet pub over there.'

She sat him in a quiet corner and fetched two double malt whiskies.

'You've told Henry that you won't go abroad,' she said,

'and I know how much you wanted to. Are you doing this partly for me?'

He grinned, wryly. 'Actually, no,' he said. 'I know what Henry says is right. Without being too egotistic, I am the best man for the job. It would be wrong of me to take skills abroad that can never be used there.'

He sipped his whisky. 'But there again, I meant it when I said I was thinking of settling down. I'm fed up with my cramped room, with meals wherever I can find them, with living out of a suitcase. I want a house in the suburbs, a wife to come home to and two-point-four children. I'll be more than happy with that.' He paused, then said, 'I love you, Lyn; will you marry me?'

'Of course I will,' she said.

EPILOGUE

SHE was happy of course, ecstatically happy. But just because he had asked her to marry him that didn't mean all their problems were at an end. They sat silently in the pub for a while, content to do nothing but hold hands. Then she took him back to her flat.

On the way they bought fish and chips again, but before they did he stopped at a supermarket and bought a bottle of champagne. 'You must drink white wine with fish,' he told her gravely. And then, shortly afterwards, they sat naked together on the bed she had made again on the carpet. They drank the last glass of champagne by candlelight.

She was sitting with her back to him, leaning against his chest, feeling his hand stroking her hair, her shoulders. 'What do we do next?' she asked.

'There's plenty to do. As soon as possible I want to go to see your parents; they should know first. Then we'll tell everybody else, and I suppose we should put an announcement in the papers. There's an engagement ring to buy, letters to write, decisions we've got to make. When d'you want to get married, Lyn?'

'Tomorrow. When do you want to get married?'

'As soon as possible. But we can't manage tomorrow; it'll have to be the weekend.' He sipped his wine, pressed a still damp kiss on the back of her neck. 'There's Christmas coming and then the New Year. I wonder if...?'

'Ross, this is going to take an awful lot of managing. Shall we just live together?'

He knew she didn't mean it. 'You want the full works, don't you? White dress, church, marquee in the garden, lots of friends. Can we get married in your parents' village? I'd really like that.'

She thought he'd read her mind. 'That's just what I want! You know I was engaged before. Well, Gavin talked about two friends and a registry office, or somewhere on a mountaintop. I don't want that; I want...' She stopped, listening to what she was saying. 'Sorry! I shouldn't have said that. And we have to decide these things between us.'

'Well, I agree with you entirely. And I don't want you to stop talking about Gavin; he was part of your life.'

'You're a kind man,' she said. 'I'm so lucky you love me. Now let's go to bed.'

'To sleep?' he asked.

For a while the department took all their attention. Christmas, New Year came and went, busy as ever. They just would not let Henry work, no matter how he said he felt better. And only when Ross tried to take over Henry's work did they realise just how much he had been doing. They needed help. And there were very few fully qualified neurological pediatricians in the country.

Then they had a stroke of luck. Lyn and Ross were studying the week's schedules when suddenly, unexpectedly, Martyn Lennard appeared in the doctors' room. He was accompanied by a vast man—easily six foot six in height, with shoulders and arms to match, and a smile as big as his body. Lyn guessed he'd be in his early fifties.

'May I present Mr Theo Harzman?' Martyn said. 'From

the Trekker Children's Hospital, Capetown, where he is consultant in Neurology.'

Lyn and Ross looked up. 'I've read articles by you,' said Ross. 'You're very good on malnutrition and its neurological effects.'

'It is one of my interests, yes. And I've read articles by you too, Dr McKinnon. I'd like to work with you for a while. To work here.'

'Mr Harzman is in London for the next four or five months,' explained Martyn, 'and he came asking if we needed an extra pair of hands.'

'Boring family business,' informed Mr Harzman. 'Wills and estates and so on; I've just got to be here. But it won't take much of my time and I like to keep busy. If you can find me something to do for, say, four days a week—then I'll start next Monday.'

'I've been on the phone, checking contracts, insurance, references and whatever,' Martyn said, 'and everything is fine. Dr McKinnon, it's up to you if you'd like a private word with Mr Harzman.'

'I think I'll take him to the canteen for lunch,' said Ross. 'I'll ring you in about an hour. Mr Harzman, you sound like the answer to our prayers.'

Theo Harzman made all the difference. He was a brilliant doctor and the children loved him. And, with their load considerably lightened, Ross and Lyn could think about getting married again. Eventually.

Some time before Lyn had applied to take Part One of her MRCS examinations in February. Henry had encouraged her to apply early and arranged a week's study leave immediately before the exam. When Henry had been taken ill, she had decided not to take the exam. There were plenty of other chances. But now Ross wanted her to go for it. 'I know only a small proportion pass first time,' he said. 'But you owe it to yourself to try. And I think you stand a good chance.'

'But what about getting married?'

'I still think it's a good idea. After the exam. Now we're going to see your parents next weekend, so let's see if we can fix a date. We'll go and see the rector at the parish church.'

'All right,' she said. 'I'd like that.'

The rector remembered Lyn very well from Sunday School, and would be delighted to marry them. He took down a thick book, and leafed through, looking at the Saturdays. 'I can't manage it before the second week of April,' he said. 'Will that do? There is no—ah—reason why you have to get married in a hurry?'

'The second week in April will be fine,' Lyn said.

It suited her parents, too. They put off a planned trip to the Sahara until the end of that month.

Ross used the management skills he was developing as next head of department to organise the event. Her parents were good, too. 'Not much difference between a jungle trip and a wedding,' her father said cheerfully. 'They're both only exercises in logistics. You leave it all to us, and concentrate on the exam.'

Lyn took the exam, and thought perhaps she'd done all right. A week later she took a taxi down to Lincoln's Inn Fields, where the Royal College of Surgeons had its headquarters. There was a list of names on a noticeboard, with a scrum of people looking at it. She eased her way to the front. There was her name. She had passed!

Next morning her elation died rather. She received a letter from Borneo, and she recognised the handwriting. It was Doug's. She didn't open it at once, but took it into work with her. She'd look at it with her fiancé.

Malcolm Saville, the surgeon who had taken Doug's

case, had kept them in touch with his progress. The operation had been a complete success, and Doug was cured. Unfortunately he felt very low, very sorry about the way he had behaved. 'I don't think it would be a good idea if you came to see him,' Malcolm had said. 'He's still feeling very guilty.'

'But there are things I need to deal with,' Lyn said. 'There's a pile of stuff here that was his brother's; I want rid of it. It's a part of my life I need to get over.'

'I'll see what I can arrange,' Malcolm said.

A week later a firm of contractors sent two men round, and Lyn supervised as they packed all of Gavin's possessions into two crates. Doug's rucksack had already gone to the hospital; the crates would be stored till he knew what he wanted to do with them. A part of her life was now over, and she was glad. Three days later she heard that Doug had been discharged from hospital, had thanked Malcolm and had disappeared.

Now a letter, from Borneo. When Ross and she had ten minutes together, she opened it. It came from the bush hospital where Doug had first been treated.

Dear Lyn,

I feel up to writing to you now. After I left hospital I came here, to the hospital where I was treated when I fell. Dr Frank Connor, the Australian doctor who helped me, desperately needed more staff. And I'm it. I'm enjoying the work, and I hope I'm giving a little bit back. I've given up climbing and the wild life; now I get my kicks out of medicine.

I hope you can forgive the way I behaved; it wasn't me. Malcolm Saville says I wasn't responsible for what I did, so I shouldn't feel guilty. But I still do. Perhaps in time the feeling will pass.

In two years I'll be back in London to take a short course in Tropical Medicine. If we could meet for a quick drink then, I'd be so pleased.

With all good wishes, Doug.

'It's a good letter,' Ross said. 'I like the man for it. Are you going to write back to him?'

'We both will,' she said, 'and all three of us will have that drink in two years.'

Time flew; there was so much to do. After a day touring the shops with Merry she decided on a wedding dress—in fact, the second she had looked at. She met Ross's brother Peter who was going to be the best man, and asked if his two little daughters would be bridesmaids. The marquee was ordered, caterers booked, local hotels asked to keep rooms for guests who would stay overnight. And all the time she and Ross were working.

March was an evil month. One day even her father panicked and rang her. 'We've just had five inches of snow,' he said. 'We'll never get a great tent up in this.' It seemed as if winter would never end. But then—it did. April bloomed, a glorious month.

Her wedding day. Bright, clear, unusually warm. She lifted up her dress, walked down the garden and was helped into an open carriage, borrowed from a local farmer. The farmer sat happily, in top hat and frock coat, behind two glossy black mares. The church bells were ringing, and old friends and acquaintances waved as they trotted through the village.

She stepped down outside the grey stone church. Her bridesmaids, helped by their mother Angela, fell in behind her, and she walked towards the church door, to meet the smiling rector.

The doors opened, to a great fanfare from the organ. She entered the church, and looked up the aisle. There, in front of the altar, was Ross. Waiting for her...

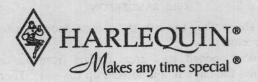

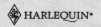

Harlequin® Historical

From rugged lawmen and valiant knights to defiant heiresses and spirited frontierswomen, Harlequin Historicals will capture your imagination with their dramatic scope, passion and adventure.

Harlequin Historicals . . . they're too good to miss!

HARLEQUIN®
INTRIGUE

WE'LL LEAVE YOU BREATHLESS!

If you've been looking for thrilling tales of
contemporary passion and sensuous love stories
with taut, edge-of-the-seat suspense—then
you'll love Harlequin Intrigue!

Every month, you'll meet four new heroes
who are guaranteed to make your spine tingle
and your pulse pound. With them you'll enter
into the exciting world of Harlequin Intrigue—
where your life is on the line
and so is your heart!

THAT'S INTRIGUE—
ROMANTIC SUSPENSE
AT ITS BEST!

HARLEQUIN®
Makes any time special®

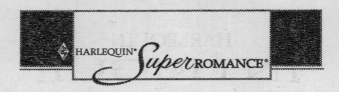

HARLEQUIN *Super* ROMANCE®

...there's more to the story!

Superromance.
A *big* satisfying read about unforgettable characters. Each month we offer *six* very different stories that range from family drama to adventure and mystery, from highly emotional stories to romantic comedies—and much more! Stories about people you'll believe in and care about. Stories too compelling to put down....

Our authors are among today's *best* romance writers. You'll find familiar names and talented newcomers. Many of them are award winners— and you'll see why!

If you want the biggest and best in romance fiction, you'll get it from Superromance!

Emotional, Exciting, Unexpected...

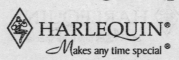

HARLEQUIN®
Makes any time special ®

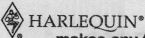